Rissa's Recovery

THE SHADOWDANCE CLUB 3

ShadowDance Club

AVERY GALE®

RISSA'S RECOVERY
Copyright © 2013 by Avery Gale
ISBN: 978-1-944472-57-3
Print Edition
First Publication: February 2013

DEDICATION

To Granny,

I miss you every single day.

You were one of the greatest gifts God has ever given me. You taught me the importance of keeping an open mind and a loving heart.

Thank you for showing me the importance of traditions and the strength that can be drawn from family.

Until we are together again......

Prologue

"CLARISSA JEAN MURPHY, you get yourself right back in there and fight. What are you thinkin', girl? It's not your time yet, you stop bein' so afraid and get on with your life. There ain't no good reason for you to keep hidin' when you have all the help in the world out there if you'll just ask for it.

"Now go on… Get yourself back there now, and you tell Brit no hurry, I'll wait for him. You get on back to livin' like I taught ya… You gotta live out loud, girl, and don't you be acceptin' nothin' less…"

Chapter 1

T HERE WAS A small part of Rissa's subconscious mind that remembered Granny was gone, *but she looked so real and young, and she sure sounded like herself, but how could that be?*

Rissa's maternal grandmother had been the most stable influence in her life, and there hadn't been a single day in the three years since she'd passed that Rissa hadn't felt like a piece of her own soul had died with the woman who had been way ahead of her time. *Hell, maybe I died and just got kicked out of heaven before I even got in. Wouldn't that top off the last two years in fine fashion?*

God, the place she'd just been while talking with Granny had been so amazing. The colors of the flowers were more brilliant than anything she had ever seen before, and the sky was the most spectacular shade blue with a depth Rissa was sure there wasn't even a word that could begin to describe it.

Fracking fudge, her head was killing her, and why was that? She didn't remember drinking anything, but her head felt like it was about ready to explode. She decided to just try to let herself sink back into the inky blackness of sleep, and hopefully, she'd feel better later when she woke up... Damn, but she wished the men standing by her bed would take a break and stop their jabbering. But then again, they did have nice voices… and they were rubbing her hand and the side of her face, and that felt so good… Maybe it would be okay if they stayed…

MITCH GRAYSON AND Bryant Davis stood on opposite sides of Rissa's bed, staring down at the fragile woman, lying too still between them. Bryant was rubbing small circles on the back of her hand as he held it cradled in his own while Mitch softly stroked the side of her face. She looked like an angel, her porcelain complexion so pale, it was almost translucent.

"Jesus, could they plug her into anything else?" Mitch's exasperated question was rhetorical, but it eerily echoed Bryant's exact thoughts. Bryant had always been awed by Mitch Grayson's special gift, but he'd understood the inherent challenges being an empath presented as well.

They'd spent many nights on the deck at Pomola, their cabin on ShadowDance Mountain, watching the river snaking its way down to the mountain valley below. Its lazy meandering during the late summer was the perfect backdrop for drinking beer and talking about anything and everything—from their views on long-term ménage relationships to Mitch's ability to hear the thoughts of people he was near. Mitch maintained not everyone was comfortable being around someone who could hear their thoughts. Hell, most people considered it a gross invasion of privacy at the least, and it just plain spooked more people than not.

"You know, when Rissa found out about my gifts, she freaked. She was going to try to stay just as far away from me as possible. I don't know yet what she's afraid I'll find out, but I know she thinks someone is after her, and I know she's scared spitless about what will happen if she's found."

Letting out a deep sigh, he continued. "We've talked about it a thousand times… Hell, we have always known it would take a very special woman, one who ignited electricity in both of us to make a long-term ménage work. Christ, I'd almost given up ever finding that woman until…" Without even finishing that thought, they both knew that woman was lying in the bed right between them.

"Letting her walk out that back door of The Club alone will haunt me until my last breath, brother." The sadness in Bryant's voice had Mitch looking up at his friend. When Bryant looked up, Mitch's eyes held nothing but compassion.

Bryant Davis had been a geeky college freshman trying to find his way around a campus larger than his entire hometown when Mitch Grayson had seemed to materialize out of nowhere with answers to questions Bryant hadn't had the courage to ask. Bryant had joked many times about how he'd wondered that day if the other man could read his mind, and as it turned out, that wasn't all that far off from the truth.

"Her beautiful green eyes sucked me right in. God, what a bonehead mistake! Christ, Mitch, I fucking know the rules, I knew what all was going down—all the extra security that was in place for the night."

Sighing in frustration and running a hand through his hair, he studied the battered woman lying too still between them. His deep voice mirrored his attraction to her.

"I nearly fell into her gaze, all I could think about was how much I wanted her, and that she obviously belonged to someone else. Fuck."

Mitch understood all too well how Rissa could scramble a man's thinking. Hell, she'd been wreaking havoc with his for months.

Rissa had been shot in the shoulder when she'd stumbled upon a clusterfuck unfolding behind the ShadowDance Club a few nights before. While the mess hadn't directly involved her, in her haste to leave the BDSM club owned by her friends and employers, Alex and Zach Lamont and housed her spa, she had wandered into a situation involving a woman she had obviously recognized and tried to assist.

The undercover DEA agent who saved Rissa's life had been shot as well, but it was the head injuries they had both suffered from their fall to a concrete surface several feet below that had been the larger concern. Damn it all the hell, she needed to wake up soon because the longer she was unconscious, the grimmer the outlook.

Mitch didn't want Bryant to know how truly worried he was—his friend was already drowning in guilt. Keeping his tone light, he said, "Hang in there… she's going to be fine. Even though the bullet is out, she'll have to do some rehab on her shoulder, but we'll have fun helping with that and the massages afterward."

Smiling down at Rissa, he was struck by how small she really looked lying there. Her personality was always so large, it was easy to forget how truly tiny she was. He knew some of the staff at The Club referred to her as Tink, short for Tinkerbell; it was an appropriate nickname.

"I have to tell you though, when she's all healed, we'll be having a serious session with her ass nicely peaked over a spanking bench. She's racked up some rather significant punishments." His soft expression and warm voice were a contrast to his words. Oh, he'd make her pay all right, but it wasn't going to be as much about punishment as it was about getting his hands on her sweet body.

Leaning down right near Rissa's ear, Mitch's voice was pitched low and full of authority, "Clarissa, you need to wake up and face the music, baby. You have some serious explaining to do. Master Bryant and I are anxious to hear what you have to say. Alex and Zach are also waiting for your explanation. If you don't come back soon, I'm going to let Katarina in here, and you don't want that do you?"

Smiling up at Bryant he said, "You haven't met Alex and Zach's pregnant tornado yet, have you? She's their wife and sub; well, at least she lets them think she's a sub." He chuckled to himself, then felt his eyes widened, a joyful grin spreading over his face as he watched Rissa's grass green eyes flutter open and her mouth twitch into a smile.

HER MOUTH FELT like she'd eaten all the stuffing out of a good-sized sofa, blah! She blinked at the bright rays of the setting sun streaming in through the window of her room. Bryant immediately closed the shades and dimmed the room's lights, so the bright light wouldn't aggravate the headache she felt beginning to snowball behind her eyes.

What the hell is wrong with the back of my head? It feels like somebody glued a rock to the it. And is that a fucking donut pillow?

Relief flooded Mitch's expression as he spoke softly to her, "Ahh, sweetheart, welcome back. We've been mighty worried about you." He was speaking to her so sweetly, and his knuckles softly caressing her cheek was the most soothing thing she thought she'd ever felt.

"C–can I have a d–drink? My mouth is so dry, and my throat feels like it's on fire." She felt tears stinging her eyes; damn, her throat was so sore, and her head was throbbing. "What happened? Where am I?" She turned her head just slightly, and when she made eye contact with Bryant, she gasped in surprise.

BRYANT STOOD PERFECTLY still and watched as her mouth formed an O, and her face flushed bright red. *Oh yeah, babe, you know exactly who I am, and that you are in big trouble. Oh, little one, this is going be a mighty fine ride, indeed.*

Bryant answered her questions while Mitch filled her cup and moved the straw to her lips. "You are in the hospital in Climax. You were shot in the shoulder, then fell off the retaining wall onto the parking area." Bryant watched her eyes dilate at his words and spark with understanding. "Sweetness, had you stayed close to The Club like you promised me you were going to do, you would not be here now." He sighed softly before he continued, "We'll be talking about that at great length later, I assure you." Bryant paused while she sipped the water, smiling when her attention finally returned to his face.

"You have given us all a very bad scare, you know. We're going to be spending some time making sure you are recovered, and then…"

Mitch Grayson's soft voice brushed over her ear, completing Bryant's sentence, "And then, we're going to be talking about all the punishments you've been racking up, Tinkerbell…" He smiled at her gasp. Just as he was getting ready to speak again, a commotion in the hall had them all turning to the door as it was flung open by a pregnant dynamo whose squeal had Rissa cringing at the pain lancing through her brain.

"Oh my God, you're awake… *Finally!* How are you feeling? Did they get you something to drink? Are you hungry? How's your head? Does your shoulder hurt? Do you need another pillow?" Rissa was certain the only reason Katarina Lamont had stopped her barrage of questions was because her husband placed his hand on her shoulder.

"Pet, you are overwhelming her. That squeal alone has probably set her head pounding. Please, give Clarissa a little space." Alex Lamont and his twin brother, Zach, were both Kat's husbands, and even though she was legally married to Alex because he was a whole two minutes older, no one would dare intimate Zach wasn't equal in her eyes. Even though she was only a few months along, she was already almost as round as she was tall, and considering she was just over five feet tall, there wasn't much room for a baby to grow any direction but straight out. From the back, she didn't even look pregnant, but oh my, from the front… suffice it to say the ShadowDance staff was already placing bets of multiples.

"What? Well, okay, but I think you're being overly dramatic… *again.*" Turning from Alex back to Rissa, she took her friend's hand in hers and just stood looking at her for the longest time before tears started rolling down her cheeks. "Don't you ever do that to me again, girlfriend! I was so worried about you. My heart dropped clear to my toes when they finally told me what had happened." Turning to glare at the men in the room before returning her gaze to Rissa, she added, "You know how they are.

They don't want to tell me a damn thing."

"Katarina… language," Alex's growling tone was negated by the tender took he gave his wife. She knew her cursing always set him off, and it was one of her favorite ways to get his attention. Kat's wink let Rissa know it had been done deliberately to lighten the mood. Kat rolled her eyes, but they were brimming with mischief.

"I'm so glad you're awake. Now, we just have to find that ornery ole Doc Woods and get you sprung out of here, so we can take you home and pamper you properly."

Doc Woods was just walking through the door and turned to Alex. "Do you always let your woman roll her eyes at you? You are a disgrace to Dominants everywhere. Pathetic, I tell ya. And you, Mrs. Lamont, are supposed to be taking it easy. I'm going to have Mitch here make a blood pressure cuff that you have to wear all the damned time. It's going to send me constant readings, and I'm going to be calling your husbands each time it's too high." Chuckling to himself, he added, "Yeah, missy, we'll see how much spare time you have for stirring up trouble then. And that reminds me, why didn't you come to my office this morning for that sonogram?"

"Sonogram?" Zach quickly stepped forward. "What sonogram? Kitten, did you forget to mention an appointment?" Even though Zach was the more laid-back of the two brothers, he had a protective streak a mile wide when it concerned his wife, and his body language was practically vibrating with barely leashed frustration.

Rissa couldn't help herself, she started giggling so hard, tears trailed down her face, and soon the entire room was laughing with her.

"Oh my God, you all are the best friends any girl could ever have. I am so lucky. Thank you for being here and just being *you*! I swear if you all had come in here all weepy and sappy, I couldn't have handled it." Grinning ear to ear, she wiped the tears from her cheeks as Doc urged everyone but Mitch and Bryant from the room.

"Now, young lady, why don't you tell me how you're feeling? I'd run these two out, but they'd just bust back in here, and quite frankly, I've gotten tired of replacing doors in this place. Damned men in this town are hell-bent and determined to know every little thing about their women." Rissa's eyes widened at the elderly doctor's words.

Did he just say their women? Oh boy…

Chapter 2

RISSA GLANCED NERVOUSLY at him, then Bryant before ducking her chin to her chest. Sighing, she answered, "I'm okay. I'm tired, and my shoulder is starting to throb, but my headache is better. When can I get out of here and go home? I have fish and a cat, well damn, unless Barney got so hungry he ate Wilma and Betty." Big tears slid down her cheeks when she thought about her pets being left to fend for themselves for so long.

"Sweetness, we have been taking care of your pets, please don't cry." Bryant's melodic voice calmed her instantly.

Mitch was standing back, watching and listening. Mitch Grayson's empathetic listening skills often allowed him to hear the thoughts of those around him. *How interesting that Rissa calms so quickly just at the sound of Bry's voice... And who did she "see" before she woke up that she wants to talk to Doc about but is holding back?*

"Doc, we'll be taking Rissa to Pomola while she recuperates. She'll have round-the-clock care. Any idea when you might spring her?" Mitch purposely ignored her widened stare when he'd mentioned taking her to their cabin, and since it wasn't up for discussion, he didn't see any point in acknowledging her confused look.

"Well, now, that does make a difference. If she was

going home alone, I'd be more inclined to keep her a bit longer, but since I know you two knuckleheads aren't gonna be lettin' her outta your sight, I'll get started on her paperwork. You should be ready to leave here within the hour." Turning back to Rissa, he added, "Clarissa Jean, you had a close call. Please listen to what these two tell you. They may be bossy bastards, but they'll have your best interests at heart, I'm sure about that."

Rissa smiled sweetly, then reached for his wrinkled hand. "I saw her… she sent you a message…" She knew she didn't have to tell him who she was talking about, her Granny and Doc Woods had been best friends and the closest of confidants for as long as Rissa could remember. She'd always felt as if their relationship was more than it appeared to be, but she'd never known for sure. She saw his eyes mist over before she continued, "She said to tell you not to hurry, she'd wait for you." Rissa squeezed his hand, and the crusty old man leaned forward and gently hugged her. When he finally straightened, it was easy to see he was trying to mask the emotion of the moment, but his soft smile betrayed him.

"I'll be holding you to that, sweetheart. I'll surely be counting on that, yes indeed." He turned and quickly shuffled out the door, leaving Mitch and Bryant staring after him.

"What the fuck was that about?" Mitch didn't even try to hide his confusion. "I've never seen Doc look even remotely soft. Hell, that was kind of scary to tell you the truth." He smiled at Rissa, then raised an eyebrow in question.

Taking a deep breath before meeting his gaze, she simply said, "It was a message from my Granny." Then, turning to Bryant, she asked, "Were you guys serious about taking me to your cabin? What about Barney? And Wilma? Oh, and Betty?" She obviously didn't have any intention of leaving her pets any longer than she already had.

Mitch sensed there was a part of her hoping he'd just told Doc that to help her get out faster, but he knew there was another part of her that was drawn to both of them. He could hear the faint echoes of a woman's voice in her thoughts... *Stop hiding... Ask for help... Live out loud...* Mitch wanted to assure her those were things he and Bryant would be happy to help her with, but she was quickly being sucked under by fatigue. Mitch smiled as he watched Rissa's eyelids slide down. She was completely exhausted, hell, she hadn't even stayed awake long enough for Bry to answer her question about her pets.

"Damn, talk about wearing yourself out. What did you make of her conversation with Doc?" Bryant's question brought Mitch back to the present.

"While she was unconscious, she saw her deceased grandmother. Her Granny practically raised her, and I know they were always very close. When she died a few years ago, Rissa went in to a tailspin... I'll fill you in on what little I know about it later. Right now, I'm interested in the messages from her Granny that were rolling around in her head just before she nodded off." Nodding toward the door, he said, "Let's step outside, we need to make some calls, and I'll catch you up."

Mitch quickly filled Bryant in on what he'd heard, and together they wondered what it might mean and how she might be planning to follow that advice. They made several phone calls, getting everything set up for the trip to the cabin. They'd already sent her cat and fish out to Shadow-Dance. There were plenty of people there to spoil the cat, and the fish were now enjoying the Koi ponds in the lushly landscaped area behind the Lamont's mansion and ShadowDance Club known as "The Gardens." Nobody thought the fish were going to miss that tiny fish bowl, but they'd likely outgrow that oversized water glass before Rissa could retrieve them.

True to his word, Doc had Rissa discharged within the hour. They'd gotten in touch with Jenna Lamont, Alex and Zach's younger sister and their friend, Colt Matthews's fiancée, and she'd brought Rissa some clothes. The next-to-nothing dress she'd been wearing when she'd left The Club had been cut off her when she'd arrived in the emergency room, and even though neither Mitch nor Bryant would have cared about taking her home stark naked, they were certain Nurse Ratched who was wheeling Rissa to the exit wouldn't have allowed it. Fuck, that woman was meaner than a junkyard dog that hadn't been fed in a week. Since they'd heard tales about this same nurse single-handedly taking on Alex and Zach Lamont, they'd decided to be accommodating and just try to get Rissa to themselves as quickly as possible.

Bryant had moved his luxury SUV under the canopy, so Rissa could avoid the light drizzle that had started about twenty minutes earlier. They needed to be getting on the road quickly before the roads iced over because as expected, the temperature was already dropping quickly. They certainly didn't want to be on the steep road leading to their retreat when the rain started turning to ice and then snow.

"Are we going to stop at my house and get some more clothes? I need some things from my medicine cabinet, too." Rissa could tell her face had turned bright red by the sudden heat that flooded her. *Damn my pale, redheaded complexion.* Sighing, she resigned herself to the knowledge she would probably never overcome that particular curse.

Mitch leaned over and whispered in her ear, "It's not a curse, Tink, your fair complexion is beautiful. Don't ever think you are less than you are because we won't allow it." He smiled at her quickly indrawn breath. "And to answer your question, everything you need is already at the cabin. We knew this was what we planned to do, so we had Jenna and Colt move whatever Jenna thought you might need yesterday. Your pets are being spoiled rotten at Shadow-Dance, so you don't need to be worrying about them, either. Matter of fact, the only thing you need to be thinking about is resting, minding us, and figuring out how you plan to explain your actions when the time comes."

He smiled, knowing he'd given her plenty to think about for the few minutes it took to transfer her from the wheelchair to the backseat. They'd loaded every pillow they'd been able to find in all three of their apartments, so by the time he and Bryant had finished packing her in, she looked like she was sitting in a bowl of marshmallows. She looked around her, giggled like a school girl, and immediately fell asleep. Damn, but she did look just like Tinkerbell, just a tiny slip of a thing, silky red curls framing her face and cascading over the pillows. God in heaven, she was gorgeous. Mitch looked up to see Bryant Davis looking at Rissa with a foolish grin he was sure mirrored his own.

"She's like a little fairy," Bryant sighed, "un-fucking-believably beautiful. Every time I touch her, it's like electricity is racing up my arm straight to my heart." Looking up at Mitch, he said, "I have no idea what it means. I've never experienced anything like my reaction to her." Mitch could tell his friend was genuinely baffled by his reaction.

"Tell me about it... Let's get a move on, I want to be sure we can get up there safely. We need this time with her if we're going to make this work, but we have a lot of puzzles to solve first." As Bryant pulled out of the hospital's parking lot and headed out of town, Mitch kept rolling all the past few days events around in his head. Thinking out loud, he muttered, "And we'll need to figure out some creative punishments for her as well."

And that is going to be no burden at all. I'm looking forward to it, and my palm is just itching to spend some quality time with her bare ass.

Chapter 3

THE PAINKILLERS THEY'D given Rissa before she'd left the hospital had done the trick, and she slept soundly all the way to the cabin. She had barely stirred when Bryant lifted her from the backseat and made his way up the steep stairs leading to the cabin. Calling the elaborate structure they'd built into the steep side of a solid rock wall a cabin was a running joke among their friends.

Incorporating elements from an old mine, they'd shored up anything they had thought might someday need the extra support, then carved and blasted away sections to make entire rooms that were lined with nothing but beautiful rock walls. All the showers were designed to look like the water was falling over the sides of the rock in mini-waterfalls, and each one had a built-in bench along one wall that had been smoothed out flat.

The hot tub was big enough to seat ten people and had been fashioned to look as if had been a natural occurrence rather than a state-of-the-art computer-controlled spa with underwater lighting and adjustable jets. The entire thing was custom made for everything from leisurely lovemaking to sexual Olympics. And damn if either of them could think of anything they'd enjoy more after their little charge awakened from her nap; too bad her shoulder bandages weren't waterproof.

After stripping her, they tucked her in the huge bed in the master suite. Since Jenna and Colt were staying at his suite above The Club while they completed the new wing being added to the mansion, Mitch and Bryant would be taking over the entire cabin. Colt had made them promise he could retain visiting privileges, particularly to the playroom, but he'd signed over his share of the cabin to Mitch and Bryant yesterday.

Colt and Jenna planned to marry on Christmas Eve, and Catherine Lamont—Alex, Zach, and Jenna's mother— was beside herself making plans. No doubt the wedding would be every bit as spectacular as the elaborate production she had pulled together for Alex and Zach's marriage to Katarina.

Catherine was a force to be reckoned with when she set her mind to something. She'd managed to turn the gardens behind the mansion and the Lamont brothers' BDSM club into a wonderland of lights for her sons' wedding. God only knew what she'd dream up for the wedding of her only daughter to a man she already loved like a son. Her husband, Daniel was a multimillionaire many times over, but he'd been recruited and quickly put to work just like every other ShadowDance employee when Typhoon Catherine had blown up the mountain to prepare for the festivities. While a part of Mitch dreaded the chaos and security nightmares involved with Catherine's huge guest lists, another part of him loved to stand back and watch the woman work her magic. And now, with Bryant home, she'd no doubt enlist his engineering expertise to create something amazing everybody would swear couldn't be done. And somehow, she'd pull it all together without breaking a sweat.

Waiting while she rested, Mitch mentally reviewed

Doc's orders and was grateful the old fart had pared down Rissa's shoulder bandages to something that resembled an overgrown Band-Aid and a sling she was only required to wear whenever her arm started to ache. The bullet had already passed through Melita Sanchez before entering Rissa's shoulder, so it hadn't done near the damage it could have.

Hell, if Mia, as she was known at ShadowDance, hadn't jumped in front of Rissa, moving them both to the side, the bastard would have nailed a perfect heart shot and Rissa would have been lost to them forever. Every time they'd talked about it, both Mitch and Bryant had thanked God for giving them this second chance, and they'd promised each other they would do whatever it took to make sure the sleeping beauty they'd tucked into the oversized bed gave this relationship every possible chance for success.

"How long do you think we should let her sleep?" Bryant had been pacing for the past half hour, and Mitch had been almost ready to shout his frustration when he'd looked up at the top of the stairs and seen her standing there, wrapped in the floral robe they'd left on the bed for her. Her hair was a mass of uncontrolled curls, wisps framing her delicate features, and her eyes were still sleep dazed, but she was without any doubt, the most beautiful woman he'd ever laid eyes on.

"I'M AWAKE, WELL, mostly…" Bryant spun around at her softly spoken words and rushed up the stairs to her side.

"Sweetness, how are you feeling? Come on, let me carry you down the stairs." He scooped her up before she had a chance to protest and moved down to the living room and sat on the sofa, positioning her on his lap so she was facing Mitch. Mitch picked up her small feet and placed them in his lap and was rubbing circles over her insteps before her mind registered how quickly they'd both managed to get their hands on her.

"Wow, I didn't even realize you'd moved. And all the sudden, I find myself down here... and... oh my God in heaven, that feels so wonderful... holy shit, I'll give you a week to stop that..." She wiggled her toes as Mitch pressed his thumbs firmly into her arches. Goosebumps raced over her fair skin, and she shifted unconsciously on Bryant's lap, rubbing her sweet ass over his erection. He fought a smile at her gasp and widened eyes. Christ, he felt like his cock was going to burst, he was so aroused just being near her.

"That's right, sweetness, that's all for you and all because you are wiggling that sweet little rear of yours all over my lap. Now, hold yourself still before I flip you over and fuck you right here on the sofa." Bryant knew his crude words surprised her. Most people assumed his quiet demeanor transferred to the bedroom, but nothing could be further from the truth.

Bryant Davis was a Dominant to the bone. He loved the power exchange of a D/s relationship and took great pride in seeing to the pleasure and care of the submissives he played with. But the minute he'd seen Rissa, he'd sensed all the other women he'd topped would fade quickly from his memory. Something about this woman electrified him. She made him want things he'd never even dreamed possible.

He'd reminded Mitch they needed to begin as they intended to go, so he intended to establish himself in a position of power immediately. Carrying her down the stairs had been as much about setting that ball in motion as it had been about conserving her strength. Every Dom worth his salt knew carrying a sub was a great way to put them in the right mindset of their physical strength, and it also provided the close tactile awareness every sub craved. In his arms, he'd been able to pull their tiny sub close to his chest, essentially surrounding her with his own body. She'd already spent months getting to know Mitch—now, it was his turn.

RISSA WENT INSTANTLY still; she knew the men wouldn't hurt her, well, not physically, but she also knew her limits, and falling for these two just wasn't in the cards for her. She'd seen too much of the dark side of men to believe in happily ever after, that was something that only happened to other women.

For her, relationships with men had always been about her giving and them taking. She'd given up on finding Prince Charming long before Dylan Marshall and his beautiful partner had walked down the stairs of Bobby Murrell's basement and found her naked in that damned cage. It had taken her weeks to regain her strength and stop smelling the stench that seemed to have become a part of her skin during those awful months. Shaking her head, she realized she'd been lost in her memories and hadn't noticed both men were just watching her. When she met Mitch Grayson's gaze, she was startled by the storm clouds darkening his eyes. There was an underlying rage brewing in their depths, and he looked ready to come apart at the seams.

"Cage? A fucking cage? Somebody put you in a fucking cage?" By the time he'd spoken the third question, he was nearly shouting, his anger contorting his handsome face. "Start talking, Clarissa. Right. God. Damned. Now."

Chapter 4

RISSA STARTED TREMBLING all over and immediately began hyperventilating. Bryant pulled her close and began smoothing his hand down her silky tresses, attempting to calm her back down. *Holy fuck, what was that all about?*

"Mitch, maybe you need to take it down a notch or two?" Looking up, he sent his best friend a scathing *back-the-hell-off-now* glare.

Bryant had no idea what his friend had heard, but whatever it was, it had sent him straight to DEFCON I status that was for sure. Slowly, Rissa seemed to be calming a bit, but her breathing was still much too shallow and fast. Bryant lifted her tear-stained face to his.

"Slow it down, sweetness. Breath in… two three and now out… two three. That's it. Nice and slow. We don't want you to faint or make yourself sick. Come on, breathe with me… that's it, good girl."

When she finally settled with her face resting against his shoulder, he felt her breath float against his neck in warm wisps of air. He noticed the change in her breathing and knew she'd fallen asleep, but he continued to hold her for long minutes simply because he was so filled with contentment. Having her nestled against him, knowing she'd trusted him enough to fall asleep in his loving care, filled a hole in his heart he hadn't even known was there. He stood up slowly, making an effort to avoid jostling his precious cargo. Turning to Mitch, he spoke quietly, "I'm going to take her back upstairs to bed and get her settled. Wait right here, we need to talk."

MITCH HAD RISEN to his feet with Bryant, but he stood as still as a statue and watched his friend carry Rissa out of the room. *Jesus, Joseph, and Mary, what the hell was I thinking? I can't believe I scared her so bad, she had a panic attack. Talk about proving every fear she had about my gifts right out of the gate. Hell, in one smooth fuckup, I confirmed the very thing I wanted to avoid!* He was pacing the room, running his hands through his hair in frustration when Bryant returned with two bottles of cold beer.

"Sit the hell down and talk to me."

Mitch continued pacing for a few minutes, downing the beer in a few gulps as he muttered to himself before he finally sat down and faced his friend.

"I was listening, and she was thinking about how she doesn't think she'll ever find love because her associations with men have not been like that... then she was remembering some asshat named Bobby who kept her in a cage in his basement until Dylan and Mia found her. I know they'd been working on a big drug case right before Dylan's cover was blown, and Mia moved on to a human-trafficking case that was an offshoot. Fuck me. I can't believe someone put her in a cage."

He'd resumed his pacing, eating up the distance with long strides. The main living area was a long room, but

Mitch was covering the distance in just a few steps from end to end.

"I'll call Dylan. I know he's taking Mia on an island vacation, but damn it, he owes me an explanation, and he can damn well give me some information, so we don't hurt her unintentionally, blundering through this minefield." With that, he stormed off toward the office, leaving Bryant gaping in disbelief.

An hour later Mitch sat on the front deck, drinking a beer, giving Bryant the lowdown on what little he'd finally been able to squeeze out of the local sheriff. The earlier storm had cleared, and the southern-facing deck with its glass windows reflecting the warm sunshine was nearly as warm as the inside of the house.

"Dylan said he and Mia had worked for months on the case, and when they couldn't get warrants to search for the drugs they knew were inside the house, he'd been convinced the judge had to be in Murrell's pocket. They caught a lucky break when they got a hot tip that Murrell was holding a woman in the house they'd been watching. Since that involved the immediate safety of an individual, they were able to enter the house without a warrant."

Taking a long draw on his beer, he felt the rage returning and wondered if his eyes reflected the fury brewing inside him.

"Dylan said they found Rissa in a cage under the stairs. She was naked and had been dangerously close to starving to death. He also noted she had a few other serious medical issues, but he refused to elaborate. Dylan said he'd tracked her progress and knew she'd recovered from all the physical abuse, but he was equally sure she's still reeling from the emotional trauma. And that is why he warned us against a public punishment for her when Jenna was paddled at The Club the night of the Annual Submissive's Masquerade."

"Do you mean Rissa was the other sub who left the spa and club that morning without a security escort?" When Mitch nodded, Bryant rolled his eyes. "Jesus, I didn't know who the other woman was, just that Colt was seven kinds of pissed at Jenna and said the other woman would be dealt with by her Dom." Looking up at Mitch's small quirk of a smile, he added, "Oh damn, you're the Dom he was talking about? Oh shit, our little pixie has a lot of punishments racked up, but I sure as hell want to know what's going on in her head before we start paddling that sweet ass of hers."

"It's time to go get her and have a heart-to-heart chat, don't you think?" Mitch was headed to the door when Rissa stepped out, wearing a pair of Mitch's boxers and a T-shirt that hung past her knees. She'd obviously taken a shower, her hair hung in a wet, loose braid down her back. When Mitch saw her, he smiled and reached for her hand. "Well, sweetheart, I was just on my way to get you. I was just telling Bryant here what I heard racing through that quick mind of yours and what little Dylan Marshall was willing to share. We'd like you to fill in some of the blanks."

When Rissa's smile melted, Bryant stepped up. "Sweetness, we don't want to cause you any more emotional pain, but we do want to help you recover. In order to do that, we need to know what we're all facing here, do you understand?" Bryant was a well-trained Dom and knew it was important to make sure a submissive clearly understood what was being requested of him or her. Punishing someone for not complying with a directive or the failure to reach a goal they didn't understand was counterproductive to building trust, and since trust was always the foundation on which all D/s relationships were built, clarification was essential.

Rissa looked at Bryant for a long moment, and Mitch sensed she was searching his face for any hint of deception or anger. From what he'd learned, she'd seen enough of both in her lifetime to consider herself an expert. When she merely nodded, Bryant leaned closer, his voice laced with steel intent.

"Not good enough, sweetness. We need you to speak your answers. Nodding and shaking your head will not be considered answering."

"Yes, I understand," Rissa's voice was clear but child soft. At Bryant's raised eyebrow, she amended, "Yes, I understand, Sir." Mitch bit back a smile at her surprise. *Baby, everybody always underestimates, Bry. You'll learn soon enough.*

"Good girl, now come over here. We've made something for you to eat while you fill us in." Leading Rissa to the porch swing, sitting her between the two of them, they handed her a small plate, then pushed off, letting the slow-rocking motion lure her into sharing some of her painful history.

Chapter 5

B Y THE TIME Rissa was finished talking, she was surprised at how energized she felt. She had never shared some of those painful memories with anyone, and she was astonished at how exhilarating it was to unburden herself from beneath the weight she'd carried for so long. When she'd finally finished and taken a deep breath, exhaling felt like she was purging the first and most difficult layer of sludge from around her heart.

She took a second, deep breath, afraid of what she'd see when she looked up at the two men who'd listened without interrupting. The relief she felt when their expressions were filled with compassion rather than pity was staggering.

Mitch was the first to speak, "Damn, Rissa, you are one brave woman. I can't tell you how impressed I am by what you've survived. Hell, I thought you were a strong woman before, but Christ, you are truly one amazing young lady."

She gasped as her heart started to melt at his kind words, then felt a grin spread over her face as Bryant reached for her hand. Giving her hand a gentle squeeze, Bryant nodded.

"You know, this whole past year while I was working on the bridge in Japan, my best friend—the man sitting beside you—has been emailing me about this incredible woman he couldn't wait for me to get home and meet." His eyes were so intently focused on her, she felt his gaze clear to her toes. His expression softened and so did his tone, "I've never known Mitch Grayson to lie, ever, and this is no exception." He turned his attention to Mitch. "Brother, she is everything you said she was... and more."

"You mean you still want to spend time with me?" Rissa was genuinely surprised and knew they would hear the surprise in her voice. Even though she felt better by venting everything, she hadn't expected them to still want her. She still felt like damaged goods and knew the issues she still dealt with might never be completely healed. Rissa had purposely avoided any close relationships because she hadn't wanted to burden anyone with the baggage that had become her life.

"Oh, sweetness, more than you can possibly imagine." Bryant's expression had turned to molten desire in a heartbeat.

Mitch's reflected the same desire. "Baby, you have no fucking idea how long I have been waiting for this opportunity. There is nothing in this world I want more, at this moment, than to sink into your sweet body. I plan to be so deep inside you, it's going to be impossible to know where one of us stops and the other begins." He smiled when she felt a heated flush work its way up her neck. Without needing a mirror, she knew her face was bright red with a combination of embarrassment at his statement and her own arousal. "But first, I believe we have a little punishment to get out of the way."

Rissa knew her face was crimson, hell even the part in her hair was probably bright red judging by how hot her skin felt. When she darted a quick look from Mitch to Bryant, he looked like he was fighting a smile but quickly masked it.

"Stand up, baby."

Rissa stood slowly, then turned to face them both.

"I–I'm scared," her stuttered words made Mitch's eyes narrow, and she wondered if he was reconsidering his attraction to her. His silence was unnerving as he continued to study her.

After a few seconds that seemed interminable, Bryant finally spoke, "Sweetness, do you believe either of us would ever hurt you beyond what you can endure?" When she only shook her head, he merely quirked a brow at her and waited.

"No, Sir," she amended quickly.

"Good girl. Now, before you lay yourself across Master Mitch's lap, what are your safe words and when should you use them?" Bryant's words were softly spoken but firm and brooked no argument.

"Red means stop that I can't handle it either emotionally or physically. When I say 'Red' everything stops for at least the rest of that day, and we have to discuss it and decide what our next action will be." She paused and took a deep breath before continuing. "And 'Yellow' means I need things to slow down that I'm getting close to things being too much, and you may or may not change how things are progressing." Amazing that she'd retained the information Mitch had briefly explained earlier, considering all she'd been through the last few days.

"Very good, sweetness. Now lay over Master Mitch's lap, he'll be giving you the first half of the swats, and I'll finish up the last half. Have you ever had a spanking, Rissa?"

Her mind started reeling and even though she'd never been spanked as a child, she knew more than she'd ever wanted to about pain. God knew the horrible treatment she'd experienced at the hands of her captors couldn't be compared to the feel of their hands warming her bare ass, but that didn't stop the black hole of fear from opening up in front of her.

"No, Sir, well, not unless you count the beatings that…" Her whole body shivered, and she started to back away from them, her eyes growing huge with fear.

"*Stop!*" Bryant's sharp tone froze her in her tracks. "First of all, little one, never back away from your Dom, especially when you are being prepared for a punishment you have earned. And second, I thought we just established that you know in your heart neither of us would ever give you any more pain than you can handle." He paused and waited patiently while she worked it through in her mind.

Holy shit, can I really go through with this? They're going to spank me. I've never been forced to lie across a lap and had my rear end paddled. She knew Kat had sworn it was worth misbehaving, just to get a spanking, and heaven knew, she'd heard plenty of other subs say the same thing while they'd been chatting in the spa. Hell, most of them swore having their pussies waxed was much more painful than a good spanking. Well, she had two choices, either pay up or safe word out and never know what could have been. Was this what her Granny had been talking about? *You gotta live out loud, girl…* She remembered the words so clearly. Taking a deep breath, her decision made, she slowly lowered herself over Mitch's lap.

MITCH LISTENED, CATCHING fragments of her thinking as

she'd sorted it all out. Damn, if she wasn't the bravest woman he'd ever known. When she draped herself over his lap, he scooted her forward, so her pert little ass was in the perfect position for his hand to warm it right up.

They had purposely let her leave her clothing on. Mitch would be baring her ass for her; there was something about only having their panties pulled down that made subs feel even more vulnerable than if the Dom punished them while they were completely naked. Mitch placed his left hand in the middle of her back, then grasping the hem of the T-shirt Rissa was wearing with his right hand, he slowly pulled it up until he could tuck it under his left palm.

When he slid his fingers into the waistband of the boxer shorts she wore, he felt her stiffen and heard her sniffle. *Fuck, if she is already crying, I'm never going to get through this.*

"You have a beautiful ass, baby, I can't wait to see it change from white to pink to red." He pulled the shorts down until they were at her knees. *God, her ass is a glorious handful of lush flesh that's going to move with the perfect amount of jiggle when my hand connects with it.*

The first swat startled her as much from the loud smack of flesh against bare flesh as the instant fire Mitch knew he'd sent skittering over the surface of her tender flesh. Her sharp, "Shit, that hurt!" had Mitch smiling. He knew it had stung, but he also knew that before the second, third, and fourth swats had landed on alternating ass cheeks, she was already feeling the electricity shooting straight from her burning ass to her clit. He could already smell her arousal, and he was only half done. Stopping for a moment to rub her hot cheeks and hold the heat beneath the surface would build her anticipation.

"Your ass is a lovely shade of pink already, baby, it's

going to be fucking unbelievable by the time Master Bryant rains his palm down on you. He has a harder swat than I do, you'll really feel his strikes. Where are we, baby? Remember The ShadowDance Club's stoplight system—give me a color." Mitch wanted to bring her back down a bit, make her refocus on the purpose of this punishment.

She was quickly starting to float, and while they didn't want to cause her any pain, this was a lesson that had to be learned. Failing to follow instructions could be—hell it *had* been—dangerous to her safety, and deliberately lying to a Dom, let alone a Dungeon Master was absolutely one of the worst things she could have done. Hell, this was going to be only one of the punishments she was going to have for *that* offense.

The ShadowDance Club's bylaws required a public punishment involving at least one of The Club's owners, the Dom responsible for the submissive, and the Dom the sub had lied to. Both he and Bryant had talked with Alex and Zach extensively on the phone about how to best proceed. On the one hand, neither of the Lamonts wanted to lay a hand on Rissa, but they knew their members deserved consistency when enforcing the rules.

It had been noted that even though the punishment had to be open to the view of the general membership, nothing in the rules stated what time it had to take place. So, they'd decided the public portion of her punishment would take place at one o'clock in the afternoon the day after they returned Rissa to The Club. At that time of day, there would be very few people present, but they would still be fulfilling the obligation of a "public" punishment.

"Rissa, I asked you a question, I want an answer. *Now.*"

"Um, oh, sorry, I'm green, Sir," her breathy response told him she had come back down a bit, but not enough.

"Tell me why you're being punished, baby. What was the first offense?" Mitch rested his hand over the crease between her upper thigh and the rounded underside of her ass, a particularly sensitive spot for most women, and he knew her anticipation of a swat there would help her focus on what was happening to her backside. He almost chuckled out loud when he saw her ass cheeks clench together.

Oh yeah, baby, I'm going to make sitting and *walking a little challenging for you, and Bryant is going to light your ass up like the Fourth of July. You aren't going to be inclined to lie to a Dom ever again once he's finished blistering your bottom, that's for sure. And Alex and Zach's paddle will keep you from sitting again comfortably for several days after we return, but you'll remember this rule forever.*

"I, um, I left the spa with Jenna, and we didn't wait for an escort like we'd been told to, oh, God, please..." She fidgeted on his lap, and he smiled when she questioned why having his hand pound her bare butt made her so horny. Mitch looked up at Bryant, his eyes widening in surprise. Hell, he'd known she was heading into subspace, that endorphin-induced "happy place" some subs slipped into under just the right circumstances, but damn, he couldn't believe she was responding so strongly this fast. *Fuck me, sex with Rissa is going to be something close to a religious experience if she is this responsive all the time.* Mitch leaned down, so his words would waft over the curve of her ear.

"Don't you fucking dare come without permission, little girl, or you are going to be in deeper shit than you already are, do you understand?" He punctuated his question with two hard swats.

Rissa cried out, then stuttered a tearful, "Yes, Master

Mitch, I'm sorry, it just, well, I don't even know how to describe it…"

Three more sharp swats cut her words off, then he quickly set her up on her feet. Hell, they were going to have to get the last half of this done quickly, or she was going to shoot off like a rocket. Neither he nor Bryant wanted to have to punish her for her first orgasm at their hands. They both wanted to be able to savor and celebrate the first time they sent her over the edge. Watching her as she felt the waves of pleasure sweep her off her feet and toss her into the deep end of bliss was something he was looking forward to.

BRYANT TURNED HER to face him and started slowly moving his hands up and down along the outsides of her thighs. Long, smooth sweeps up and then slowly back down until she refocused, and they knew she'd come back from the edge.

"Now, sweetness, tell me why you are getting a punishment at my hand when I would much rather be sinking my aching cock into your wet pussy. I can see your sweet cream glistening on your swollen folds, pet. You are the picture of temptation."

At Rissa's deep blush, he added, "Don't you dare be embarrassed by something that is beyond amazing. Your pussy recognizes its Masters even if your mind isn't there yet. Your sex is practically pulsing with need. Now, answer my question, so we can get this punishment over with and give you that orgasm your body is craving."

Bryant knew his crude words would either push her

closer to the brink or pull her back, and he was anxious to see which it would be. Her reaction would tell him a lot about her comfort level with not only this punishment scene, but also how well she was converting the pain into pleasure. It had always amazed him how closely the brain processed two sensations that seemed to be at opposite ends of the spectrum. The reality was the brain was easily fooled, and for most true submissives, certain levels of pain quickly changed to intense feelings of pleasure.

"Sweetness, why am I going to paddle this ass I'd rather be fucking?" Bryant's harsh tone had the intended effect, yanking her back from the brink and helping her focus.

"I lied to you the night of the Submissive's Masquerade." She immediately lowered her gaze, not in submission, but in genuine repentance of her deeply felt guilt.

He'd known she really did feel bad about what she'd done. Bryant was relieved because now, he would be able to back off the intensity a bit. While it was important to get the message across, if a sub was already remorseful, a punishment that was overly harsh would have the opposite effect the Dom was striving for.

"I'm really sorry, I don't know what I was thinking, and as soon as I walked out the door, I knew I'd really messed up and I..." Big tears filled her eyes, spilling over and running in streams down her deeply flushed cheeks.

"Let's get this over with, sweetheart. Lie over my lap." Bryant had never wanted to just call off a well-deserved punishment before this moment. Damn, this little sub was already burrowing herself deep into his heart. Settling her into the correct position, he palmed her heated flesh and delivered the first five swats in quick succession, never landing two consecutive slaps in the same spot, making sure he spread them out. Likely, she was going to have a very red bottom for the rest of the night and wouldn't be sitting comfortably for a couple of days, and that was fine. Her discomfort would serve as a well-deserved reminder.

Hell, every time he even thought about the danger she'd put herself in, he got pissed all over again. And every time he thought about the fact he'd made such a dumbass mistake, he wanted to beat his head against the fucking wall. They could have easily lost her that night. He gave her a few seconds to settle down, but then delivered the last five, fast and hard. Dammit, if he didn't do it quickly, he'd fold, and when all was said and done, she *needed* this lesson.

By the time he finished, she was crying so hard, the wracking sobs were making her entire body tremble so hard, he worried she might shake apart. He lifted her easily, cradling her in his lap, rocking her back and forth. He kissed the top of her head and praised her for how well she'd taken her punishment.

Bryant was self-aware enough to know the motions and words of comfort were as much for his benefit as hers. Fuck it all, he'd wanted to call it over after the first set of five, but a Dom's word had to be golden or there would never be any real trust between the Dom and the sub. And without trust, there was no D/s relationship in the world that could survive.

Mitch had watched closely as Bryant delivered the last of Rissa's punishment, then tenderly care for her after it had ended. Bryant hoped she hadn't whitewashed out, and his friend was able to listen in on what was tumbling around in her head. He couldn't help but feel her crying was more a catharsis of emotion than just an ordinary reaction to a chastisement. It was doubtful Mitch would be able hear much through all the emotion—feelings that intense tended to cause what Mitch had described as a sort of psychic-static. The only thing he'd ever been able to compare it to was static electricity's effect on radios. The signal was still there but was being covered up by a layer of something more intense.

It seemed to take her forever to finally begin to calm, Bryant had been close to taking her in to the shower to shock her back into focus. He wouldn't have used the river because it was much too cold this time of year for even a quick dunk. He smiled to himself thinking about the times they'd dropped sweet little subs into the cold water as either punishment or reward during the warm summer months. Even though the air was warm during the summer, snow melt made up the largest portion of the river's flow, so it was never anything you'd want to spend a lot of time splashing around in. But the water was always crystal clear, and the view of the rocky bottom of the riverbed from the cabin's deck always made him think Mother Nature had created a perfect mosaic of Colorado's finest geology for their enjoyment.

They'd often talked about how great it would be to replicate the design, creating a stone patio but had never had a space to do it. Perhaps he'd remind Colt; he and Jenna might be able to use it in their addition to the ShadowDance mansion. Bryant gave himself a mental shake to clear his head and corral his wayward thoughts. He needed to focus on establishing a bond with the little sub cuddled in his lap. The time after a punishment was critical to the establishment of trust, and he'd allowed his thoughts to wander. He really needed to get his head back in the moment.

"Come here, baby. I need to have some of this cuddle

time, too." Mitch's voice brought her head up and he took her hand and helped her stand before moving her onto his lap, wrapping his arms completely around her, and burying his nose in her sweet-smelling hair. "Oh, sweetheart, you smell so good, like fresh citrus and lush woman." Mitch ran his hand up her thighs and into the leg opening of the boxers they'd pulled back up. Bryant saw his friend's smile and knew what he'd found. "Oh my, you are soaking wet, I think someone enjoyed their spanking."

Bryant leaned back and sipped his beer as Mitch ran his fingers through the drenched folds of Rissa's pussy. He heard her soft gasp just before she whispered, "Please..."

Chapter 6

T HE MEN QUICKLY moved Rissa inside to lay her out on the enormous bed in the master suite. The bed had been specially made to easily sleep four larger-than-average-sized adults. They'd designed and built with polyamorous relationships in mind. It was also the perfect height for bending a sub over to paddle or fuck their lovely ass. The four posts at each corner were sturdy enough to use in suspension scenes, and best of all, there were eyebolts and open spaces disguised within the ornately carved head and footboards where scarves, ropes, and chains could be used for bondage games.

Before she was even completely settled, they had her stripped and were standing back, just looking at her with the strangest expressions.

"What's wrong?" she finally managed to eke out. When they didn't respond, but just continued to stare at her, she moved to the edge of the bed preparing to leave. Obviously, they'd seen something that changed their minds. "Look, it's okay, I know I'm not in the best shape, and I have some... um... well, scars and stuff... so don't worry about it, okay?" She wouldn't look at them, she wasn't sure she'd be able to keep from falling apart if she saw repulsion or worse yet, pity in their eyes.

"*Stop!*" Bryant's deep voice and sharp bark made her

freeze. Rissa was so locked in place, she was barely even breathing. "Look at me now." The command had her slowly raising her face until she was able to meet his gaze. She gasped in surprise at the raw desire she saw burning in his eyes. "Come to me, sweetness, I want to show you what Mitch and I see."

Bryant grasped her hand and helped her from the bed, walking around to the ornately framed mirror mounted on a rolling pedestal. Standing behind her, he could easily look over the top of her head.

Rissa didn't know when he and Mitch had removed their shirts and shoes but seeing them both reflected in the mirror had her gaping at what she saw. *Holy shit, they are both pure sex on a stick. Oh my God, and I thought they were hot before. I want to run my hands, hell, I want to run my mouth over every inch of those hot bodies.* Rissa looked up and saw Mitch's wicked grin and raised eyebrow. *Oh, fuck a duck, I forgot he can hear what I'm thinking, but sweet Mother of God, I don't care. I just want me some of that!*

Mitch's snort of laughter was the first time Bryant had broken his gaze from her delicious body. Mitch looked at Bryant and explained, "She thinks we're hot." Rissa appreciated that he hadn't repeated everything. Damn it, the recap alone had been embarrassing enough. She could see the bright red flush staining her cheeks; if he'd repeated it all, she probably would have glowed in the dark for a week.

Bryant's slow, sexy grin seemed to light him up from the inside. Rissa knew both men were really handsome, but Bryant's smile literally took her breath away.

"So, sweetness, you like what you see?" Bryant's voice was low pitched, and she'd noticed it seemed to lower even more when he became aroused. When she only nodded her head, he practically growled. "Not good enough, pet; we will always require you answer all questions promptly and with words when we are in a scene, particularly when we are in the bedroom."

Mitch leaned close to her ear. "And you need to always answer honestly, baby. You'll be required to answer every question with complete honesty. In a relationship like the one we'd like to build with you, there is no room... *ever*... for holding back or lies. Dishonesty dishonors your Doms and yourself, and it will be severely punished. Don't forget that." He was so very close, his warm breath wafting over her ear caused her to shiver. "Now, answer Master Bryant's question, baby."

"Yes, Sir. I like what I see very much. You are both incredibly good-looking men." Rissa barely recognized her own voice, it sounded so airy and soft. God knew, she had never been known for being soft-spoken; she couldn't count the number of times her Granny had reminded her of the importance of speaking "like a lady," whatever the hell that meant. Bryant's arms encircled her, his large hands touching her breasts with gentle strokes until she'd answered, then he pinched her nipples hard, and she gasped and tried to jerk out of his embrace.

"Ouch, what the fuck? Why did you do that? I answered you honestly." She glared at him in the mirror in defiance.

Bryant's smile immediately disappeared. "That's five swats for language and five for disrespect, sweetness. I wanted to know if you liked what *we* are seeing. Remember, we are standing here instead of giving you the orgasm of a lifetime because of your disparaging comments about our property. And don't think for a single minute you aren't ours. This beautiful body belongs to Master Mitch and to me." Skimming his hand down her torso to slide his fingers through the drenched folds of her pussy, he held his fingers up for her to see they were shiny with her juices.

"See this? Your body already recognizes its Masters. You are so beautifully responsive, I can't wait to sink in until my balls are slapping your sweet ass. But now, we need to get these swats done. Turn around and bend over the bed. Present your ass for punishment, pet."

Rissa's eyes filled with tears almost immediately, and it didn't have anything to do with fear of the pain. No, she felt bad for disappointing them, and she knew she had let them down, but she really had misunderstood the question.

Jesus Christ, Rissa, keep quiet, these two hot men want you—at least for tonight—take what you can, and you'll have some great memories to relive after they move on. She knew she wasn't the type of girl hot guys kept around, and there was no way on earth she had a prayer of keeping two guys satisfied.

BRYANT WATCHED RISSA'S expression go from lust to defeat in a split second, but he was completely baffled by the change. Looking to Mitch for help, he saw his friend's grim expression and knew he was listening and not at all happy with what he was hearing.

"Rissa, stand up and look at me. Right now!" Mitch's barked order had her standing immediately, but she didn't lift her eyes to meet his. He placed his fingers under her chin and forced her to look up. Bryant watched as his friend searched their little sub's expression. "Tell me why you feel so unworthy, baby. Who fucking told you that garbage? I swear to you they are dead the minute I get to them because crushing another person's spirit is one of the worst offenses you can commit."

Mitch's sincere words obviously touched her heart, and Bryant breathed out a sigh of relief, grateful beyond measure for his friend's special gifts. Bryant stood watching as Mitch continued.

"You are an amazing and beautiful woman. Sure, you're going to make mistakes and be punished for them, but that doesn't mean we are disappointed in you as a woman. D/s relationships have rules for a reason, they are for your protection and pleasure. Sweetheart, if we allow you to think badly of yourself, we are *not* doing you a favor. We want you to see the beautiful woman we see and desire. You are being punished, so the next time you start to make a negative remark about yourself, you'll remember these stinging swats to your already-tender ass cheeks, and hopefully, you'll stop before you make the same mistake again. Over time, we'll be able to show you how gorgeous you are, and those thoughts will fade to an unpleasant memory." He stroked away the tears that had fallen. "Now, turn around, spread your feet shoulder width apart, and bend over."

Rissa bent over the bed and felt Bryant move her feet farther apart before he laid his palm at the small of her back and pressed down.

"Flatten your back, sweetness; that will cause your ass to rise perfectly." When her heart-shaped ass was perfectly displayed, he brought his hand down hard for five fire-evoking slaps that had her crying out in pain. As soon as he landed the last blow, Mitch took his place and gave her another four hard strikes. His last swat was less severe but landed directly on her pussy, making her entire body quake.

"This body is beautiful. Don't you ever say anything negative about what belongs to Master Bryant and myself. Is this clear?" Mitch was determined to make sure she understood exactly how pissed he was about her negative self-image, and Bryant was in total agreement. They'd be exploring that bullshit further... later, but not right now. Right now, if he didn't fuck her, he was going to explode.

"Yes, Sir. I'm sorry, Sir," Rissa's sobbed words were spoken more like a prayer than a true apology, it was obvious she needed release, and they were just what the doctor ordered.

"Up on the bed with you, sweetness. Now, are you on birth control?" Bryant wanted to forego condoms if at all possible. He hated the damned things with a passion but hadn't taken a woman bareback since he was fifteen years old.

Rissa hadn't moved but answered quickly, "Yes, Sir. My doctor's report is on file at ShadowDance." Suddenly, her voice dropped to a mere whisper, "And I haven't had sex in... um, well... a while, so I'm clean." Rissa immediately looked away from their inquiring gazes.

"Exactly how long is a while, baby?" Mitch was trying to hear her thoughts, but she was so aroused he wasn't getting anything.

"Well, um, oh boy... you probably aren't going to want me after I tell you this, but, um, well..."

MITCH WAS QUICKLY losing his patience. "What were the

rules about answering, Rissa? Repeat them to me."

"I'm to answer honestly and immediately. I know. I'm just, well, it's embarrassing to admit I haven't ever had real sex before." She kept her eyes down and for a few second, Mitch was grateful she'd disobeyed because she'd missed their identical looks of surprise. He watched and listened to the thoughts streaming through her head.

Hell, I was supposed to be sold as a sex slave a couple of years ago and here I am, a twenty-six-year-old virgin—how humiliating.

Mitch and Bryant both stared at the red-haired beauty standing in front of them with a mix of emotions swirling between them. Bryant found his voice first.

"You mean you're a virgin? Holy fuck that's incredible. You're truly going to belong to us in every way." He grabbed her and gave her a rib-crushing hug before turning her to Mitch.

Mitch lifted her chin and kissed her on the forehead before speaking, "Baby, this is the most beautiful gift you could have ever given us, and we'll cherish it always. Being your first is an incredible honor." He kissed her with a depth he hoped she felt to the very bottom of her soul. His tongue searched her mouth, testing her for every possible reaction, and when she melted into his embrace, he felt like his heart was going to explode.

When he finally pulled back, he looked at Bryant who nodded. The unspoken communication told Mitch that Bry agreed Mitch should go first. Even though his cock was slightly longer, it wasn't quite as thick as Bryant's.

"Now, move up onto the bed. That's right, get right in the center... Now, let us love you, baby. We were going to fuck you, but now? Well now, we want to make love to you. This is a moment we'll all remember for the rest of our lives, and we want to make sure the memory is just as sweet as you are." He moved up alongside her, playing with her soft folds, running his fingers through their wetness, just barely dipping his fingers inside her sweet channel before moving forward to circle around her clit, then tracing the same path again. Bryant had moved to her other side and was using his tongue to tease her nipples into sharp peaks.

"That's right, sweetness, we're going to make sure your innocence is surrendered in a way that fills you with all the joy and wonder of lovemaking. The gift you're giving us is beyond measure. I can't begin to tell you how honored I am to receive it. For tonight, the only rule you need to remember is to be honest with us at all times."

Mitch smiled knowing Bryant was pressing the peak of her nipple between his tongue and the roof of his mouth, making her arch closer to him and moan his name. Mitch was being flooded with pleasure radiating from both Bryant and Rissa.

"Oh God, Master Bryant, that feels so good... it feels like there are electric pulses going from your mouth all the way to my pussy. It's amazing."

Watching Rissa as they overwhelmed her with so many sensual sensations at the same time was sending so much of Mitch's blood to his cock, he hoped his brain would function well enough to hold him back. The last thing he wanted to do was hurt her by rutting her like a desperate animal.

In no time at all, she was squirming and tilting her pelvis up, trying to get the relief her body was screaming for. Moving over her, Mitch placed the head of his engorged cock at the entrance of her pussy and slowly started working his way in, inch by tight inch.

"Oh, baby, you are so fucking tight. And wet. And so hot, your sweet pussy is going to burn me to a crisp. Try to relax your muscles and let me in, I don't want to hurt you." Mitch felt the beads of sweat forming on his forehead from his effort to hold back and not thrust in balls deep.

When he reached the thin membrane barrier, he stopped.

"Look at me, Rissa, I want to be able to look into your eyes when I claim your virginity. Remember this moment and how much I love and desire you." Before she could even process he'd just told her he loved her, he pushed through and sunk so deep, his tip was pressing against her cervix.

Mitch groaned with a level of pleasure unlike anything he'd ever experienced before. He couldn't help the emotions that swamped him, and knew in that instant, he'd been right all along. This was the woman he and Bryant had always dreamed of finding. *Oh my God. Heaven itself can't possibly feel this good. I'm never letting her go. She is* mine*!*

When Rissa gasped, he knew she'd felt a pinch of pain as he'd pushed all the way in. He'd felt her tissues stretching around him and knew the intense feelings of being filled were quaking through her when he felt her rippling around him, but she quickly lifted her hips in invitation. Thank God, she wanted more because he wasn't sure he'd have been able to walk away from the dizzying pleasure of feeling her skin to skin. It was obvious she wanted him to *move*, and he was happy to oblige.

"Oh please, Master, please, I need you to move. I have this amazing feeling starting to build up, and I don't want to experience it alone… Oh my God. Oh my God. Oh my God… what is that?" Rissa's words were being spoken so fast, it took Mitch a second to sort them through.

"Oh, baby, *that* is your G-spot—we'll often call it your sweet spot. Like that, do you?" He tilted his hips, so he was bumping it with each stroke. He was quickly building up a rhythm, and just when he didn't think he could hold back another second, she exploded around him. Her pussy walls pulsed in tightening bands squeezing his cock nearly to the point of pain and pulling him over with her.

He followed her over the edge into a deep canyon of pleasure, and he wasn't sure he was going to survive the fall. He felt his cock shooting his seed against her cervix, and his inner caveman wanted to beat his chest in triumph. When he finally caught his breath enough to speak, he framed her face between his huge hands.

"Oh my God, sweetheart, that was amazing. You touched my soul, Rissa." He kissed her sweetly, then slowly withdrew from her body's tight hold. Bryant handed him a warm cloth and he lovingly cleaned Rissa's tender tissues. Her eyes were drifting closed, but his words seemed to bring her back.

"Oh no, baby, no sleeping yet. Bryant wants to make love to you, as well. Give him the gift of your body. Show him the pleasure you just shared with me." He moved off the bed going into the master bath to clean himself up and heard Bry talking softly to Rissa as he walked away.

"SWEETNESS, I CAN'T tell you how hot that was to watch. Now, up you go. I want you on your hands and knees if your shoulder will allow it. Your pussy is going to be swollen from your recent orgasm and lovemaking, and this position is going to make us both enjoy this experience even more. That's it, lean down and put your head and shoulders on the mattress. Let me help you spread those amazing legs farther apart, then I'm going to take you back up that peak quickly, love. I got so hot watching you and Mitch, I'm not sure how much control I'll have."

He slid himself between her sensitive folds, absorbing the warmth of the engorged petals of her labia before slipping further inside. As soon as he was fully seated, he started long, smooth strokes, hitting her cervix with each thrust. Rissa's body responded immediately, and Bryant heard himself softly moaning her name. He was bowled over by the depth of their connection.

"Oh, sweetness, your pussy feels unbelievable. It's like a steaming hot, wet, velvet glove squeezing me as it tries to keep me inside. The ripples rolling over my cock are making me quake with desire, I can't wait to feel you come all around me."

Tilting his hips just a fraction, so he hit her sweet spot with each thrust, he sent her flying before either of them realized she'd reached her peak. Screaming out his name as she bucked back against him, he heard his own deep voice shout, "Fuck… Ah, babe, that's it, take it all!" The pleasure of feeling his hot seed spurting deep inside her core sent her into another orgasm before the first had even begun to subside.

Dropping completely flat onto the bed, Rissa was gasping in a desperate attempt to catch her breath as Bryant withdrew and collapsed on the bed beside her. After a few minutes, he cleaned her with a warm, wet cloth Mitch handed him. He was grateful to see her so replete, she didn't have the energy to protest.

Mitch was lying beside her, finger combing the strands of her hair back from her face, brushing soft kisses over her temple and closed eyes.

"Sleep now, baby. You were amazing, and we are so proud of you. You are everything we dreamed you would be and more," Mitch's voice was almost hypnotizing, and Bryant watched in satisfaction as Rissa let herself sink into an exhausted sleep.

Bryant slipped from the room to clean up and returned to stretch out on her other side. Drawing small circles with his fingertips over her lower back, he smiled when goosebumps raced over the surface of her fair skin.

"She's fucking amazing. She's the woman we have looked for all these years. I can't believe we've finally found her," his voice was quiet, more from his tone of reverence than from a deliberate effort to not disturb her.

"All those emails you sent—I was so certain you were exaggerating because I knew we were both beginning to feel like we were searching for someone who didn't exist. But when you started sending the pictures, I couldn't wait to get home. There is an ethereal quality to her... I don't even know how to describe it."

"I know exactly what you mean. It's like God listened to our descriptions and created her just for us. Now, all we have to do is help her overcome her fears and convince her we are here for the long haul, so we can collar and marry her." Looking up, Mitch's slow smile almost convinced Bryant that he had it all worked out. "Piece of cake."

Chapter 7

RISSA MARVELED AT the care and affection Mitch and Bryant had lavished on her the past few days. After she'd gifted them with her virginity, they seemed to coddle and care for her even more than before. They both took great pains to help her learn all the rules of D/s relationships and the various points of protocol she would need to perfect before they'd allow her to play at The Shadow-Dance Club. Their patience with her "form" and her utter lack of control when it came to controlling her orgasms had been more than she could have asked for.

They took great pleasure in paddling her ass when she acted out, then sliding their fingers into her, demanding she come the minute the last strike landed. They hadn't let her wear one stitch of clothing since that first night, insisting they wanted unfettered access to "their property," and access it they did... on the kitchen counter, over the lounger on the deck, leaning over the sofa, even in the bathroom while she'd tried to brush her teeth. She'd lost track of how many orgasms she'd had. Now, she stood looking out the large front windows watching the first snow of the season as the flakes drifted lazily toward the ground, covering everything, and quickly turning the landscape into a winter wonderland.

"Penny for your thoughts, baby." Mitch's strong arms

encircled her, pulling her back against his broad chest. God, she felt so safe in his arms, while she was with Mitch and Bryant, she could almost forget she was still in hiding. There was a part of her soul that was certain the sex-traders who had kidnapped her would never give up.

Staying in tiny Climax had been an obvious solution in the beginning because everyone knew everyone else, and strangers stood out immediately. Since the local sheriff knew her story, he was always on the look-out for anyone who might be a potential threat to her. She could almost convince herself she could stay here forever rather than knowing it would all end when she was finally found.

Rissa had always known she would eventually have to leave the only true home she'd ever known. Leaving Climax and all her friends was going to break her heart, and she had the feeling the other shoe was getting ready to drop… the underlying fear had been bubbling up inside her for several weeks now.

"Why do you think you have to run? Talk to me, Rissa, we want to help. We don't want to lose you."

Turning to face Mitch, she looked up in to his compassion-filled eyes, and the tears she'd been trying to hold back breached her lower lids and slid silently down her cheeks. Leaning forward, he kissed them away, pulled her into his chest, and just held her for several minutes, hoping she'd regain her composure.

When she couldn't seem to settle herself, he told her he was worried she was going to make herself sick as he scooped her up into his arms and moved to the sofa. Mitch looked down at her and spoke quietly.

"Alex and Zach have talked about having to spank Katarina before a scene, just to settle her racing thoughts and help her regain her focus. She is a very bright woman whose quick mind doesn't shut down easily. Is that what you need, baby? Do you need help with your focus, so we can get to the bottom of this?"

It took Rissa several seconds to comprehend what Mitch had said. She saw Bryant enter the room, standing to the side with his arms crossed over his massive chest, looking like a sentinel in a wet dream. Both men were barefoot. God help her, their feet were so sexy, she loved when they moved around the house in nothing but a faded pair of jeans with the top button open. *Sex on a stick for sure.*

"I... I don't know... I just feel overwhelmed right now."

BRYANT STEPPED FORWARD and nodded his agreement to Mitch. Their little sub needed them to help her get back to center, and they'd be happy to provide the small slap of pain that would get her where she needed to be.

"Bend over Mitch's lap, sweetness, and let us help you with your little focus problem."

As soon as she was over Mitch's knees with her rounded ass in the air, they spread her legs apart just enough they'd be able to slide their fingers through her pussy and push her over the edge. They'd decided to push her a bit, starting today, and she'd just handed them a free pass to begin. Pulling the lube he'd stuck in his back pocket free and laying it on the table out of her sight, Bryant watched Mitch give their woman an erotic spanking that had her panting for release before he'd finished the fifth slap. Her ass was a nice warm pink, hell, it had been pink or bright red most of the time they'd been at the cabin. They'd tried to be careful not to bruise her delicate skin, but she'd had some bruising yesterday, so they would have to be more careful today.

Bryant moved to separate her ass cheeks, and when she jerked in surprise, Mitch pressed her back down firmly with a hand at the middle of her back.

"Shhh, stay still. We're going to start preparing you to take us at the same time. In order to do that, we need to stretch this beautiful rosette of yours." As he started rimming her with a finger slicked with her own juices, Rissa went completely ballistic, bucking so hard she knocked herself off his lap, landing hard on her knees on the stone floor. She was completely hysterical, screaming and running from them like a terrified wild animal, making sounds that couldn't even be called words.

Mitch immediately jumped up from the sofa, but when he met Bryant's baffled expression, he knew the other man was as confused as he was.

"Rissa. Stop. Now." Even though Bryant had used the Dom voice she always responded to, he didn't think his words had even begun to penetrate her panic. Mitch finally appeared to be listening, before turning to Bryant and mouthing the word, "flashback."

Bryant's heart seized, and he could tell by Mitch's expression he was thinking along a similar track… she hadn't told them everything about the time she'd been held by the human-trafficking assholes.

"We've got to flank her and get her restrained before she hurts herself. As soon as I have her secured, go get the med kit, there is a syringe filled with Ativan. Bring it to me, we have to get her calmed down."

Rissa was running around the room as if trying to escape a cage she couldn't even see. She was running into the low tables, and Mitch knew Bryant was as worried as he was she would be bruised from head to toe if they didn't get her contained quickly. While she had adrenaline on her side, they had years of physical training and size on theirs.

As soon as they had her face down on the sofa, Bryant brought the med kit and handed the small-dose syringe to Mitch. It didn't take but a few seconds for the drug to course through her veins. Rissa's breathing evened out, and they felt her go lax as she succumbed to the sedative action of the medication. They'd given her a very small amount of the drug that was a part of the med kits all soldiers carried because they didn't know exactly how she'd react to it, but they hadn't been able to leave her in her state of total meltdown, either.

Mitch stood and gently rolled her to her back, brushing her sweat-soaked hair from her face and wondered aloud, "What the fuck was that about? I was totally blindsided by that reaction."

Bryant leaned over and scooped her up in to his arms. "I have no idea, but it scared the shit out of me. Call Alex and Zach. See what they know and have them contact Doc Woods. I'll take her to the bedroom and watch over her while you try to find out what we need to do. I don't ever want to see that look of terror on her face again. And knowing we triggered it nearly shattered my soul."

Mitch reached over and grasped his shoulder and squeezed. "No, brother, whoever terrorized her is responsible for that reaction. Our responsibility lies in helping her heal." He turned and quickly made his way to the office, and Bryant could hear him already speaking with Alex before he'd carried his precious cargo to the top of the stairs. Leaning forward to kiss her forehead, Bryant marveled at how perfect she felt in his arms.

"You were made just for us, sweetness, and we're going to help you recover from this, then we'll build a wonderful life together. No one will ever hurt you again, please let us love you well."

Placing her gently on the bed, Bryant tucked her against him, covering them both with a soft throw and just held her close, so he could feel each beat of her heart and every breath she took. He absorbed her warmth and let his mind drift in to a state of relaxation while he waited for Mitch to return to them.

MITCH SPENT OVER an hour on the phone with Alex and Zach Lamont. They'd called several PTSD experts to confer via a teleconference call and gotten as many different theories and suggested courses of action as possible. Not surprisingly, it was Katarina Lamont who had finally barged into her husbands' office and into their conversation who offered the most useful advice and insight.

"I'm telling you... I've been where she is... you just have to spend time with her. The only way to overcome her fears is to love them away." While Alex and Zach had not been happy with her intrusion—they were going to superhuman levels to shield their beautiful wife from anything and everything while she was pregnant—they both looked oddly touched by her words. "Holding her, talking to her, and above all, *listening*—and I mean really hearing what she's saying—is what she needs. Well, that and a girls' gab session with my famous margaritas, but since that's not on the table at the moment..."

Glancing at the glares she was getting from both Alex

and Zach, she smiled sweetly and returned her attention to Mitch's image on the monitor.

"Seriously, Mitch, I'd love to come over to the cabin and help, but with the weather the way it is, I'm sure I won't be allowed to leave the house." Sighing deeply in the dramatic way she was quickly elevating to an art form, she finished with, "But please, please listen to me on this one. Love her, listen to her, and we'll do some checking on this end to see if there is any other treatment that's recommended. Jenna and I talked about this a while back, and we were worried she's been holding back. We'd actually planned a mini-intervention of sorts after the wedding. I just wish we hadn't decided it could wait." When tears started to roll down her cheeks, Zach stepped forward and wrapped her in his arms.

"Come on, kitten, that's enough for now. If Mitch needs anything more from you, I'm sure he'll call. Let's get you upstairs for a bit of rest, okay?" His voice was soft and filled with compassion, but there was no doubt in anyone's mind Kat was on her way upstairs to rest despite her protests.

As they left the room, Alex watched, muttering about her being his entire reason for living as his brother escorted Kat out of the room. He returned his attention to Mitch.

"Honestly, I think Katarina might be right, and she certainly has a unique perspective. I'll make some more phone calls. There are a lot of PTSD experts around, but in the meantime, please try what my lovely, sweet-spirited wife has suggested. We all know she has Rissa's best interest at heart and handling her with love is certainly not going to cause any harm even if it doesn't solve the problem."

After he and Alex had ended their call, Mitch realized he'd been sitting, just staring out in to the darkness watching the swirling snowflakes dance in the moonlight. *What did they do to you, baby? Whatever it was, nothing is so bad we can't work it out. You'll never be so far gone emotionally that Bry and I won't swim out and pull you back. Hang in there, sweetheart, we're on our way…*

Chapter 8

JENNA AND COLT made their way slowly back up ShadowDance Mountain's narrow, winding road, grateful for the tire chains and their four-wheel-drive vehicle. They'd been in Denver for several days, making the arrangements for the contents of Jenna's apartment to be moved as soon as weather allowed. They also stopped for supplies on the way back when the weather reports become more and more grim.

Colt broke the silence and filled Jenna in on the conversation he had with Alex and Zach while she'd been packing up some personal items in her apartment.

"Rissa had what appears to have been a very traumatic flashback. Mitch and Bryant had to restrain her and administer a sedative."

Jenna's eyes widened to the size of small saucers. "Oh my God, is she okay? Do we need to go to the cabin and help? Oh, I wish Kat and I hadn't put off talking with her. We've been concerned that she was teetering on the edge, and we'd decided to wait until things settled down a little before trying to get her to open up to us." Jenna was wringing her hands and biting her bottom lip, both major tells as to her anxiety level. Colt knew she and Katarina would both be empathetic toward Rissa since they'd been through really horrific experiences themselves.

He let his expression soften and looked at her for just a second before returning his gaze to the blizzard conditions surrounding them.

"Slow down, princess. First of all, we're going to the mansion, and I want to get you settled and rested. I know it's been a challenging week." When she opened her mouth to argue, he just continued, "No, I mean it, I want you to rest, then after that, we'll sit down with Alex, Zach, and Katarina and see what we can do from our end to help. Rissa is important to all of us, pet, and we'll get her through this. Please don't worry about it right now. With the move, getting ready to start school, and wedding plans, you have plenty on your plate." He winked at her when he mentioned the wedding. She wasn't sure who was more excited about their upcoming wedding and all the elaborate plans, her fiancé, or her mother. Personally, she thought it was probably a toss-up.

Sighing, Jenna looked out the window, but Colt didn't think she was really seeing anything and she spoke so quietly, he wasn't sure if she was talking to him or herself.

"I've been where she is. Flashbacks are just so devastating, and there isn't any way to explain to someone how it feels. The terror is all consuming… it's like being right back in that moment all over again." She visibly shuddered, and when she turned back to Colt, he was just putting the truck into park. Jenna looked up, appearing surprised to see they'd arrived at her family home. She'd been so lost in thought, she hadn't realized they had driven past the front gate and up the long-winding drive.

Colt reached over and unlatched her safety belt and pulled her onto his lap, hugging her tightly to his chest. "I love you so much, Jenna, and I don't want you to ever feel like you can't come to me if you are hurting or if something in your life is causing you discomfort."

Brushing away her tears, he watched her eyes widen in surprise. She hadn't even realized they were falling, and once again, he realized the depth of her compassion for others. Kissing her forehead, he whispered, "I'll always be in your corner. I'll be your biggest advocate, your champion, and your knight in shining armor. All you have to do is make sure I know you need me, and I'll move heaven and earth to be there for you. Don't ever forget that, love." He hugged her tightly once more before opening the door and carrying her quickly inside.

OF COURSE, KAT was standing just inside, waiting for them and wrapped Jenna in a hug as soon as they were through the door. Jenna laughed to herself as the woman who'd been her best friend forever and was now she was her sister-in-law tried to maneuver around her growing belly. Kat looked like she was trying—unsuccessfully—to hide a beach ball under her shirt. She would never say anything to Kat, but she was starting to remind Jenna of a Weeble. *Great, now I'll have that damned Weebles Wobble, but they don't fall down jingle stuck in my head forever!*

As usual, Kat was in full-on fast-forward mode. "Come on, we have to talk. Did Colt tell you about Rissa? We have to figure out how to help. How was your trip? Did you get everything you were after? Thanks for getting supplies by the way, you're a lifesaver." Suddenly, she realized everybody in the room was openly staring at her. "What?" she asked, her face reflecting her puzzlement.

"Love, I think we are all wondering how you do that

without stopping to take a breath. It's incredible. Really— even if you're overwhelming Jenna." As always, Alex seemed to be amazed at his wife's ability to think of so many questions in succession and ask them in a rapid-fire manner that would make the most seasoned White House reporter proud.

Alex continued his calm words, "From what Colt told me, he would like for Jenna to rest a bit before your strategy session, and Zach and I are going to insist on the same for you." Drawing his little sister away from Katarina, he gave her a big hug.

"Welcome home, little sister mine. I'm thrilled you've decided to move home, did I tell you that?" At her slow head shake, he added, "Well, Zach and I are both thrilled we'll all be living under the same roof again. We love you and want to be able to help Colt protect you. God knows it's going to take all three of us working together to keep Lucy and Ethel out of mischief." His smile was so unexpectedly soft, his expression filled with tenderness, Jenna almost cried. Was this the same hard-assed brother she'd grown up with? Zach had always been her shoulder to cry on and her champion. Alex had been the one she went to if she wanted to know how to knock somebody out or if she just felt like arguing.

Smiling at him, she hugged him back. "I love you, too, big brother, married life has been good for you." Then looking at Zach, she added, "You two are going to make great dads. But, me? I am going to be the world's best aunt… you just watch and see!"

Then she moved over to hug Zach. "I love you, too, BB Zach," she said using the nickname she'd called him as a toddler, it had stood for "Big Brother Zach" even though she often substituted "Big Bear Zach" because she'd always considered him her cuddly teddy bear brother. It had never mattered to Jenna that Alex and Zach were literally mirror images of each other, in her eyes they'd always seemed completely different. She'd never understood why other people weren't able to tell them apart. Finally, Jenna turned to Kat.

"I'll see you soon, sweet sister, but right now I'm beat, and frankly, this is a battle I don't have the energy to fight nor do I particularly want to win." Smiling at Colt, she let him take her hand. They all agreed to meet after dinner in Alex and Zach's office before Colt led Jenna up to her suite.

As Colt walked her up the stairs, he placed a chaste kiss on her lips and whispered, "Well handled, princess. I do believe you have a reward coming." Jenna smiled up at him through her thick dark lashes.

"Thank you in advance, Master." *Great gads, am I going to get a nice pre-nap orgasm or what? Hooray for me!*

Chapter 9

RISSA BEGAN TO surface from what she sensed had been a drugged sleep. *What the hell happened to me?* For just an instant, she started to panic, but as soon as her hands fisted the silk duvet on the bed, she knew she wasn't back in the cage. Immediately, roughened fingertips were brushing the hair back from her temples in gentle caresses, and as the fog cleared from her mind, Rissa realized someone was speaking in soothing tones close to her ear. She wasn't awake enough to fully comprehend the words, but the tone of his voice was almost hypnotizing, and the whisper touch of his fingers through her hair calmed her more than anything else could at that moment.

Bryant knew the instant Rissa started to come awake. Even though he'd been sitting across the room working on his laptop, out of the corner of his eye, he'd noted when her muscles tensed and her breathing hitched. He'd been at her side in an instant and wasn't at all surprised to see Mitch standing at the door less than a minute later.

Mitch's gift of empathy would strengthen as his bond with Rissa grew. Mitch had explained it to Bryant in detail over the years, and the nuances of his friend's ability never ceased to amaze him. Bryant knew Mitch had been outside moving wood into the bins near the fireplace, but that growing bond would have alerted him when she had started to surface from the sleep of the dead. They'd decided to only use the fireplace and candles for light this evening, hoping to keep Rissa in a state of calm reflection. They needed to spend some time listening to her, and they intended to make it as stress free as possible for her.

While they had appreciated the support they'd gotten from Alex, Zach, and Colt, it had been the words of wisdom from Katarina and Jenna that had made the most sense. Keeping his voice low, he asked, "How is she?" Until Rissa became more aware of her surroundings, Mitch wouldn't be able to hear much, but he was feeling the slight increase in her energy.

"She just started to stir but was sliding into a panic." Bryant hadn't changed his tone of voice or altered his touch while he answered. Sighing at the sight of the beautiful woman lying before him, he whispered, "I don't care what it takes, she's worth it. We'll help her through this and build a life with her." Looking up at Mitch's smiling face, he knew his best friend was completely on board.

"Isn't she the most amazing woman you've ever met? I have been trying to get to this point for the past eighteen months. Hell, I knew she was perfect for us even before you left for Japan but couldn't get her to give me the fucking time of day. It took me months to get her to even say 'Good morning' to me!" Mitch chuckled as he remembered all the days he'd spoken to Rissa only to have her duck her head and dart out of the room.

"And dinner was pure torture; she would respond to questions others asked her but religiously avoided any form of contact with me. Her thoughts would race, and all she was focused on was escaping my presence." Sighing and running his hands through his hair in frustration, he continued, "That is one of the main points I want to work on tonight. I want to know why, and I want to begin building a foundation of trust."

RISSA HAD BEEN listening and was being steamrolled by her overwhelming feelings of guilt. Mitch Grayson had been beyond patient with her, and she'd hurt him with her own fear and insecurity.

"I'm sorry," her whispered words drew both men's attention immediately.

She felt Mitch move closer and saw him kneeling by the bed when her eyes fluttered open. His soft lips grazed her temple before he spoke. "What are you sorry for, pretty girl?" She sighed and tried to focus on his face, but the tenderness in his eyes made her vision blur as tears filled her eyes.

"For being so rude to you when you have been so kind and patient with me. I never considered I might be hurting you." Taking a deep breath before continuing, her voice had become so quiet, it was almost as if she was thinking out loud. "I was so busy worrying about myself, I... well, I was just being selfish, and I wasn't raised that way." Rissa tried to smile but suspected she hadn't fooled them.

SMILING DOWN AT her, Mitch watched her expression change like the clouds of a turbulent storm. "Well, in that case, apology accepted. Now, let's get you up and downstairs, so we can feed you. We have a wild and crazy evening planned, and we wouldn't want you to miss out on a single minute of firelight staring, now would we?" Mitch took one hand as Bryant grasped the other, and they helped her from the bed. "I'll see you both downstairs. I have a few things to finish up."

Mitch knew it was important for Bryant to have time alone with Rissa. They'd spent years planning how to share a woman in the kind of permanent relationship they were now trying to establish with Rissa, so it wasn't hard to know when to push and when to pull back. Mitch and Bryant would ensure Rissa understood it would never be about "equal time," and it certainly would never be her responsibility to keep track of the time she spent with either of them. The planning would always fall on their shoulders.

Knowing this was just one of many things they wanted to discuss with their woman this evening, Mitch made his way to the kitchen and loaded the trays with all her favorite foods and began moving them in to the living room. He hoped tonight was the first of a lifetime of evenings spent enjoying one another's company.

Rissa and Bryant were sitting in the living room, facing the fire by the time Mitch brought in the last tray with their filled wineglasses. Rissa was wearing a peacock-colored silk wraparound robe; they wanted her to be as comfortable as possible while they talked.

"You look beautiful, baby, that color looks great on you. Did Bry tell you he brought it back from Japan just for you?"

He'd sent Bryant hundreds of pictures of Rissa during his year-long absence from ShadowDance, so his best friend hadn't had any trouble knowing what would look great with her porcelain skin and rust-colored hair. Rissa's cheeks went instantly bright pink, damn, she was adorable when she blushed.

"Well, I see by that sweet blush, he did."

"Yes, he did. Thank you both for it, it feels amazing. I love the silk, but I've never owned anything that feels this luxurious before." She'd been absently rubbing the fabric between her thumb and forefinger, and that small tell hadn't escaped his or Bryant's notice.

Bryant leaned forward and kissed the tip of her nose. "Sweetness, you are a beautiful woman. You are *our* beautiful woman, and we'll take great pleasure from giving you everything your heart desires, and even many things you'd never think to ask for." His sexy grin told Rissa he was talking about a lot more than just clothing. "Mitch and I both make a lot of money, and we've been investing it wisely for a very long time. We'll enjoy spending money on you, and you will honor us by graciously accepting our gifts."

They had already anticipated she would be resistant to accepting expensive gifts, so he'd decided to head her argument off at the pass. Rissa's naturally submissive nature would lead her to decisions and choices she knew would please her Masters as long as they could keep her listening to her heart. They knew the problems would all come from her tendency to overthink things.

After a couple of glasses of wine, they were all relaxed, enjoying the snacks and the joy of one another's company when a loud beeping from the office had Mitch on his feet before Rissa had barely been able to blink.

"What's that?" Rissa's voice reflected the tension she'd picked up from Mitch's instant reaction to what sounded to her like an alarm.

Mitch didn't answer her, but looking at Bryant, he merely nodded.

"Sweetness, that is one of the perimeter alarms. We aren't expecting any company, and we'd like to check it out." Mitch was already moving, and Bryant was essentially pulling her down the hall right behind him. "We hadn't wanted to introduce you to our playroom quite this soon, but it also serves as our safe room, so I'll ask you keep that in mind as we cross this threshold."

"WE HAVE TO go to a safe room? Why can't we just answer the door if they make their way up to us? They might be lost. It's so cold outside, what if they need help?"

Rissa wasn't even going to think about the horrible threats her captors had shouted at her as they'd been led away in handcuffs two years ago. As far as she knew, they were all still in jail, awaiting their trials or had been convicted of lesser charges and were serving long prison sentences in federal facilities back east. As if the Universe had heard her thoughts, Mitch's cell phone rang.

"Talk to me." Mitch's clipped tone told Rissa all she needed to know... *Keep up and keep quiet.* The tension radiating off both Mitch Grayson and Bryant Davis felt like waves crashing over her. "What the fuck do you mean you just now realized the connection?... Seriously?... When did you get the notification?... Well, get somebody out here ASAP. We've had a perimeter breach, and we're going into lockdown... Keep us posted." Mitch dealt with the conversation and never lost a step, he was clearly back in a military mindset, preparing and assessing seamlessly.

Bryant looked at his friend and raised his eyebrow in silent question. Mitch's head shook almost imperceptibly. Her three glasses of wine fueled her bravery, and she dug in her heels and fisted her hands on her narrow hips before speaking forcefully.

"Well, don't clam up on my behalf, geez, Mitch, I'm not made of glass, and we all need to know what we're up against here."

Rissa felt herself starting to slide into panic and was sure it was as much because they weren't telling her what was happening as it was that someone had broken through one of their "perimeter moonbeams." Kat had coined the term for what she viewed as the security-overkill mentality that seemed to pervade all the men at ShadowDance. Personally, Rissa had always thought the security was a bit overdone too, but more often than not, she merely chalked it up to "soldier boys with cool toys."

Turning to Bryant, she stayed planted in place. Moving her feet shoulder width apart, she made a show of crossing her arms under her ample breasts, completely unaware of how she'd put them on display for both men to see. She stood there, scowling at them both.

"You know something you aren't telling me, and I'm not going anywhere until you do."

Bryant leaned over, put his shoulder in her stomach, and lifted her effortlessly. "Oh, but, sweetness, you most certainly will do exactly as you are told, and you just earned yourself a nice paddling for that little display of defiance."

Even though she gasped in outrage, her traitorous body was giving her away by flooding in anticipation, a reaction she doubted he'd miss since his nose was danger-ously close to her pussy. She knew he hadn't been fooled when he ran his fingers up the insides of her thighs and found her wet enough to slip a finger deep inside.

"Don't even try to tell me you don't like the idea of being bent over my lap with your bare ass burning under my palm, pet, because you are creaming at just the mention of it." Bryant's words were stern, but she could hear the underlying humor.

They entered the playroom, and Rissa was unceremoniously dumped on the large bed in the center of the room. When she started looking around, she was amazed to see how much it reminded her of the main lounge at Shadow-Dance, but with a medieval-dungeon-meets-cave twist. The equipment was beautifully crafted and polished to a brilliant sheen that filled the room with the smells of rich leather and lemon-scented polish.

One wall was entirely rough-cut rock, owing to the cabin's history as a former mine. The natural springs working through the rock fed into a hot tub that had various levels of smoothed rock surfaces, no doubt used for water play. The hot tub was huge, and Rissa could see there were lights and jets concealed in the rock walls, and she couldn't wait to use it. She had always loved water and relaxing in water as it swirled around you was about as good as it could get in her opinion.

She watched as Mitch put his hand to a small panel on the wall and gasped in surprise as the wall slid aside and another room appeared.

"Holy shit, this looks like some kind of NASA control room. You guys really take this security business way too seriously, you know that? Jesus, Joseph, and Mary! Can you launch nuclear weapons from this place? Damn, does the government know about you guys? Oh shit, what am I saying? Of course, they do... they trained you fools... this is insane."

Mitch didn't particularly like what Rissa was saying, but he was more concerned about the rising panic he heard in her voice. He hadn't wanted to scare her, but obviously her imagination was doing a bang-up job of that all on its own. He turned to her just long enough to make eye contact.

"Rissa, that phone call was from one of Dylan Marshall's deputies. They received a notification one of the men who held you hostage has jumped bail and absconded. The agents who searched his house found a note with your name, address, and cell phone number. Likely, they have traced your phone to this location." He saw her eyes widen and felt the wash of cold fear he knew he was picking up from her emotions.

"STOP! Don't let yourself fall over that edge, Clarissa. We need you to be with us right now. We're going to bring up the outside cameras, and you're going to help us figure out who we're dealing with."

Mitch had known the only way to keep Rissa from spiraling into debilitating fear was to make sure she had a role to play. He knew her well enough to know she was a submissive through and through even when she fought it. As a true submissive, she would set aside her fear to serve a Master she respected and even if they hadn't yet established the deep bond they were working toward, he knew she had a firm foundation of respect for all the Doms at The Club.

Bryant knew immediately what Mitch was up to and had to hide his smile. God, but it was fun being a Dom and watching another Master play a sub like a song. He was all in on the plan.

"Rissa, you'll be a very valuable asset, please stay put until we have a chance to get everything lined up, all right?

We'll have you move over here as soon as we're ready for your help." Knowing she would be completely compliant when she felt she was "helping" played heavily in their favor, and it would keep her calm and quiet while they ran the sophisticated face recognition software that would tell them everything they needed to know about the intruders. They didn't want to run the risk of triggering another flashback and wouldn't use her unless they absolutely had no other choice.

From their peripheral vision, both Bryant and Mitch could almost see Rissa's demeanor change as she slipped quickly into the mindset of a sub. Her softly spoken "Yes, Sir" was confirmation of the body language shift they'd seen. Bryant looked at Mitch and smiled, thinking, *She's fucking perfect for us.* Hearing his thoughts as he knew Mitch would, he watched his best friend nod before returning his attention to the monitors showing every corner of their property.

Chapter 10

MITCH AND BRYANT had been watching the monitors for several minutes when she saw Bryant tap the one directly in front of him, studying it closely. Rolling his chair closer, he began typing furiously on the keyboard and talking on a hands-free radio headset she hadn't even noticed he was wearing.

"I've got them, Sector 1 about a hundred yards out and closing fast, they're on snowmobiles." He tapped the earpiece and continued. "Jantz, Creed—wire 'em up… yeah, yeah… play with 'em, but don't kill 'em." Smiling, he looked over at Rissa. "Ethan and Jamie want to play. A bit of cabin fever. You know how they are."

Mitch knew the grin he flashed her made him look like the ornery boy he'd been growing up. Rissa released a breath she probably hadn't realized she was holding, and he was forced to return his attention to the screen.

Zooming in on the intruders, he growled, "Oh yeah, you asshats, come on in…" The next time he looked at her, he was pleased to see she'd lost some of the deer in the headlights look she'd had when they first brought her into the saferoom. Her posture was more relaxed.

Bryant seemed to understand the risk of triggering a flashback was outweighed by her anxiety at being left floundering in the unknown. as he turned to her and said,

"Come here, sweetness. Let's watch the boys play with these assholes. It'll be fun..." Bryant scooted back from the console and patted his lap.

He settled her, so she was facing toward Mitch and tapped the inside of her thigh, indicating he wanted her to part her legs. "Master Mitch is working, but that doesn't mean he doesn't want to see you. Open your pretty robe and keep your legs spread."

Mitch had to shift in his seat to relieve the pressure on his rapidly inflating cock as Rissa slowly untied the sash and let the robe gape open. When she slowly moved her legs apart, Bryant gave her exposed nipples a quick pinch. "I'm sure Katarina and Jenna have told you about the rules they follow at dinner every night, and since you'll be doing the same, you might as well get used to this position, pet."

RISSA KNEW HE was referring to the fact her friends always wore dresses or skirts to dinner at ShadowDance. She'd heard them comment numerous times about not being allowed to wear panties and being required to sit with their legs spread wide apart with their feet hooked around the outside of the legs of their chair. Anyone paying any attention at all could see Kat's and Jenna's men enjoyed the benefits of their vulnerability every evening. She'd watched both Kat and Jenna freeze, their eyes close as their lips compressed tightly together, and their whole-body shudder in release. The most significant thing she'd noticed about all the Doms at ShadowDance were they never went more than a few short minutes without touching their sub, and she'd always envied that close physical connection. She'd often wondered what it would be like to have that kind of constant bond, that continual positive reinforcement of touch. Before the trauma of her kidnapping, she'd been a very tactile person, but afterward she'd dreaded being touched by anyone. Mitch and Bryant had been the rare exception, but she still felt the old fears try to surface from time to time.

BRYANT KNEW SHE was seeing her friends' obvious pleasure in her mind's eye, and he loved her shiver of realization as it raced up her spine. *Oh yes, pretty girl, you are completely exposed to Mitch's view.* Rissa's legs spread even farther apart as a natural response to the appreciation she saw in Mitch's eyes, making both men smile. Bryant ran his hand lightly along the inside of the thigh pressed against his abdomen.

"Very good, sweetness, listen to your body because it recognizes its Masters, and that makes both Master Mitch and me both very happy."

"Baby, you are gorgeous," Mitch added, "and looking at your glistening pussy is making me so hard, my cock is throbbing. As soon as we get these yo-yos taken care of, I'm sliding into you and fucking you for hours. We love touching you, and we'll be happy to bring that joy back into your life." He'd slid his chair over, close enough to drag his fingers through her soaking folds, then lifted his fingers to his mouth and sucked them clean. "You taste like sweet honey. We're going to lay you out on the table and feast on you after we warm up your sweet ass for that little show of defiance in the hall, of course." He smiled at her gasp, then returned to his work.

Bryant didn't say anything to her for long minutes as he continued to tease her with callused fingers. They watched two people in snowsuits and face masks as they neared the area close to the cabin, and Rissa jumped when, all of a sudden, they were thrown backward, and their rides continued without them until the lack of pressure on the throttle brought them to a stop.

"Wow, did they hit something at the same time?" Rissa wasn't sure she would be able to concentrate on the answer with Bryant's fingers lighting her up from the inside out, but she felt an obligation to at least try to participate in what was happening.

Mitch chuckled as much at knowing how she was struggling to concentrate as the comedy unfolding on the monitors. "Damn those two are having a great time out there. This is what they live for." At Rissa's puzzled expression, he explained, "Ethan and Jamie have been itching for some action for a couple of months, this is right up their alley, and these intruders are amateurs, or they would have at least gotten close without being detected."

Shaking his head, he zoomed the camera in as the intruders were being cuffed and their masks removed. One of the others pulled out a device and appeared to snap pictures, then type furiously on the handheld device before loading the prisoners onto snowmobiles and disappearing again into the woods. Almost instantly, the images started loading on Mitch's screen, and he began working furiously on his keyboard, his fingers fairly flying over the keys.

Bryant slid a finger just inside Rissa's pussy. He knew she might be able to conceal a reaction on the outside, but it took a very well-practiced liar to suppress the body's internal muscle contractions.

"Sweetness, do you..." He didn't even get the question

out before he felt her internal muscles clamp down on him like a vise, but rather than attempting to draw his touch closer, she was trying to retreat. Her breathing quickly become little more than shallow panting. He watched the base of her throat as her pulse rate became erratic. Looking at Mitch, he raised his brows.

"Well, I don't think there is much question our woman knows at least one of these men." He turned her face to meet his gaze, effectively breaking the connection to the pictures. "Tell us, pet. Who do you see?"

Rissa was barely breathing, and Bryant knew she was probably already seeing little black spots in her field of vision. Bryant removed his fingers from her pussy and turned her quickly, framing her face with his hands forcing her to look into his eyes.

"Breathe with me, pet, I know you practice yoga, so in through the nose for one, two, three and hold for one, two, three and out for one, two, three and again…" After a few cycles of cleansing breaths, Rissa's focus seemed to return, and she nodded.

"Yes, I recognize them both. One was the man who drugged me, and the other was the one who seemed to be in charge at the house where I was held." She shuddered, and Bryant wrapped his arms around her.

"You have done so well, we are so proud of your courage." Bryant's words were simple, but they warmed her from the inside out. "I'm sure they didn't give you their real names, so we'll be using our resident genius' facial recognition software to get those. So, for now, we'll be spending some time making sure you let that mind of yours take a break. See, that's one of the joys of being a submissive, you get to let go and just feel. You won't have all those 'I should have… I could have… I need to…'

thoughts cluttering up your consciousness. You get to turn all of that off and let us lead you to peaks of pleasure you never knew existed."

Rissa was so mesmerized by his words, she hadn't even realized they had all three moved to the playroom's oversized bed. They laid her in the center and fully opened the robe she was wearing, so it fell to her sides. Mitch lowered his lips to hers, and just before they touched, he whispered.

"You are so fucking amazing, smart, brave, and so beautiful, I can barely believe you are ours. And make no mistake, Rissa, you are ours, we'll spend the rest of our lives reminding you exactly why surrendering your body and heart to us was the wisest decision you ever made." He proceeded to kiss her with what could only be called a total oral seduction.

She'd been kissed by men she considered good at setting the mood, but this was a whole new level of intensity. It seemed as if he was trying to draw her soul out of the dark where it had been hidden for so long. It was intense but not overpowering. When he finally let her go, he caressed the side of her face with a gentle touch that belied the fire in his eyes.

"You bring a joy to our lives that is really beyond my ability to even describe, baby."

Mitch turned her toward Bryant who kissed her forehead and her eyelids before plundering her mouth. His kiss was so much more "in your face" bold, that she was momentarily startled, but he was relentless. She hadn't really considered the two best friends would have such starkly different styles, but it seemed they both held separate keys to her deepest thoughts and desires, the very essence of her. When Bryant finally let her surface, she was practically vibrating with pent-up energy.

"What's going through your mind right this minute, sweetness?" When she hesitated, his voice took on a sharp edge of command. "Pet, I'll remind you we are your Masters, you will answer every question asked of you immediately and with total honesty. Now, tell us what you were thinking."

"Oh, well, I was just thinking about... well..." She took a deep breath, straightened her shoulders, and then looked directly in his dark eyes. "I was just thinking that you have such different styles of kissing, different paths to seduction, yet it's like you each have a different key to the same lock. You each have a different way to reach the very deepest depths of my soul." Rissa noticed Mitch moved closer to her, and Bryant's eyes softened.

"Baby, you are the most amazing blessing; I can't begin to tell you how much that means to me." Mitch's hands were stroking all around her bare breasts but missing her tightly peaked nipples begging for attention.

Bryant looked at her for long seconds before adding, "Please always be as honest as you just were with us. I'm honored and humbled; you have no idea how much those words mean to us both." They immediately began what could only be described as making love to her soul. Rissa hadn't had any real firsthand sexual experience, but she wasn't without a basis of comparison after listening to her clients' detailed descriptions of D/s play for the past year and a half. And this was far beyond anything she'd heard described or seen in a D/s relationship at ShadowDance or anyplace else.

"I don't understand..." At their curious expressions she said, "Oh, I'm sorry, am I supposed to ask permission to speak?" She really hadn't thought about it, and she knew she was probably tromping all over the rules of the lifestyle they were introducing her to.

Bryant was the more alpha of the two Doms, so he would take the lead when Rissa had questions. "Until you are more comfortable with scenes, we'll make sure you know what protocol is required. We won't ever punish you for breaking a rule you didn't know about. Even though we are both Doms, and I am deeper in the lifestyle than Mitch, we'll all work together to establish the rules and parameters of our relationship. This will only work if we are totally honest with each other and trust each other implicitly. It is important to us that you feel free to ask your questions unless you are specifically told to not speak."

Mitch caught her chin with his fingers, turning her to face him. "Baby, we want this to work, so we're going to do everything we can to make sure it's a positive learning experience for you. We'll teach you with firm hands, guided by love. Never doubt how important your happiness is to us. We'll have a lifetime to observe high protocol during specific scenes, but tonight? Tonight, is about making sweet love to the woman who has taken over our hearts."

His eyes reflected the love he had just put into words, and Rissa was amazed it didn't scare her spitless. She had been convinced she wasn't lovable to anyone anymore, that her time in that basement cage had siphoned something elemental out of her.

It was obvious to Rissa they were finished talking. She could almost feel the energy in the room shift, and she knew that change was enough of an answer for now. They enveloped her and used their hands and mouths to set every square inch of her body on fire in a seduction that rocked her to the foundation of everything she thought she knew about herself. She'd known they could be tender, gentle lovers, but she had no idea they could touch her with such tenderness and in ways that made her believe in forever. It felt like a merging on a level of intimacy she had never even allowed herself to imagine, let alone had the opportunity to experience.

They worked together seamlessly to lead her to a place of pure pleasure. Feeling their hands smooth over her skin lit up every one of her nerve endings. She felt electric need arcing along the surface, then tunneling directly to her breasts, clit, and pussy. For just a moment, she wondered how it was possible that a tongue tracing along the arch of her foot could send pulses of need to her nipples. She tried to track their movements and figure out who was where because she wanted to make sure to give them equal time.

Bryant saw Mitch lift his face from Rissa and tilt it to the side as he often did when he was working to hear the thoughts of the person near him, one of his friend's very few tells. Mitch smiled and left the bed briefly to retrieve a silk blindfold from the lingerie chest on the other side of the room.

"Baby, you are spending too much energy trying to keep score. It isn't your job to make sure you treat us equally, that responsibility is solely ours. We don't want you to ever feel guilty about spending time with us individually. As a matter of fact, we'll be arranging that regularly. It will be important to us that you are open and honest with us about your needs. We are fully aware we'll be fulfilling different needs for you, and we're looking forward to you getting to know us and exactly what we can do for you, both individually and together. But for now, right now, I'd like to blindfold you, so you'll stop worrying and let us lead you." Mitch watched her closely, using every skill he'd ever learned as a Dom to make sure there was not a trace of apprehension in her expression. "Do you trust us, baby?"

Rissa didn't even hesitate. "Of course. I trust you both, and I want to overcome the past, and I know it's going to take time and patience… but I… well, I really want to chase the horrible shadows out of my life… and I know I can't do it alone."

BRYANT WAS HUMBLED, knowing the brave and beautiful woman lying between them had just given them the greatest gift a woman could give a man, her trust. Rissa took his breath away in so many ways, he wasn't sure he'd ever be able to list them all. When he finally spoke, he had to work around the lump of emotion lodged in his throat.

"Your trust is a gift beyond measure, pet, and we'll work the rest of our lives to prove it was a decision you need never regret." He knew his words weren't the most eloquent, but they were spoken straight from his heart, and he hoped that was enough to carry the message through.

As Mitch secured the silk over her eyes, he watched the pulse at the base of her neck speed up, but he obviously hadn't sensed any anxiety because he'd given Bryant a devilish grin. Bryant knew anticipation and excitement would add to her experience, but they didn't want her to be truly fearful. A bit of apprehension would heighten her senses and make the pleasure more intense. They were anxious to show her all the ways her body could experience pleasure.

Smiling over at Bryant, they easily fell into well-practiced hand signals to keep Rissa from being able to track them by their voices. They'd be talking to her, but they wanted to make sure she was so lost in sensation by the time they did, she wouldn't be worrying about the "scoring" problem she'd been caught up in earlier.

When Bryant set his mouth to her pussy, thrusting his tongue deep inside without hesitation, he felt her muscles tighten over his tongue, and he flashed on the thought he had never wanted a woman as much as he did at this moment. Every single sexual experience he'd had was a small step leading him to this woman and this relationship. It was incredible to realize she was the woman he planned to spend the rest of his life with, and he could barely contain his excitement.

As Bryant elicited sighs from their woman by using his mouth to work his magic on her sex, his best friend drew her nipples deep into his mouth, pressing them against the roof of his mouth. Watching her arch her back, trying to get closer and giving Mitch even greater access was a vision in sensuality.

She had a body that was as close to perfect as he'd ever known. Their woman wasn't stick thin, she had an amazing hourglass figure that reminded him of a pin-up girl. It would be a pleasure to grip her curvy hips as he fucked her tight ass; he could hardly wait to introduce her to that pleasure. He knew she had minimal experience with ass play, so even though he was anxious to feel her shatter around him as she experienced the orgasm he knew they could show her, he also knew she would have to be carefully prepared. Unless she was properly stretched, it wouldn't be a pleasant experience at all.

Mitch tuned into Rissa and smiled when he sensed her

awareness of the fire building inside. Everything they were doing to her was stoking the flames, but nothing was quite enough. *Perfect.*

"Please… I need…" was all she was able to get out before she sank back into a level of desire that blocked her ability to think clearly or articulate those feelings.

Listening to her inner dialogue just about broke his resolve. *Holy Mother of God, these guys are amazing, I'll lose my mind if they keep this up.* He knew she sensed his shift and probably felt his lips curve into a smile against her aching nipples, but right at this moment, he was grateful she was too lost in the rush of pleasure to make herself to care enough to question him.

Bryant was torturing her pussy with his devil-blessed mouth and a tongue she decided was nothing if not pure magic. Even though she couldn't see them, Mitch was pleased she'd learned their touch and knew which man was where, or at least, she thought she did.

When Mitch sensed she was tumbling into a haze of pure lust, it was time to move. Spreading her legs wide and bending them at the knees, Bryant pressed the tip of his cock against her entrance and began pressing through the tight tissues. Mitch smiled when he felt the pleasure she was experiencing as the burning of stretching tissues gave way to the joy of being completely filled with a hot cock. Her self-narration as her vaginal muscles contracted and pulsed was a gift he hadn't expected, and he grinned when he heard Bryant's low growl.

"Oh, my fucking God, she's already rippling around me and milking me. I'll never last if you don't hold back darlin'."

"I'm sorry… but I can't seem to control it." She tried to still herself, both inside and out, but her body wasn't listening to her mind. "I want you both, but my body is just pushing right past what my brain is trying to dictate."

Mitch sensed her struggle because she could already feel the first wave of an orgasm building, and she was trying valiantly to hold off. She knew she wasn't supposed to come until they'd given her permission. He almost burst out laughing when he heard her start reciting multiplication tables. She started doing mental math and thinking about old Mr. Van Meter her algebra teacher. Evidently, she'd liked him, but hadn't considered him sexy, and the brief mental picture he got of an older man who looked a lot like Albert Einstein confirmed he wasn't a crush made Mitch smile.

Just as she thought she might be gaining ground of her control, Bryant shifted his hips and the angle of his thrusting, so he was hitting her sweet spot inside with every stroke, and she broke over the edge, screaming her release, her muscles clamping down so hard, Bryant cursed and followed her almost immediately.

Mitch watched as Rissa blew right past her own and Bryant's control. He'd never known Bryant Davis to lose control of his release, hell, the man's restraint was legendary among Doms and subs alike at The Club. Mitch had seen Bryant work over *two* subs restrained in stocks one night in the main playroom at ShadowDance, wringing multiple orgasms from both experienced submissives before he'd allowed his own release.

Knowing Rissa had been able to shake what everyone considered Bryant's unshakeable mastery made Mitch smile and earned him the middle finger from his best friend. Mitch slid his mouth down, so his tongue was dipping in to her navel as Bryant slid his still semi erect cock out of Rissa's warmth. Mitch continued his sweet perusal while Bryant retrieved a soft, warm, wet cloth and gently cleaned Rissa and then himself.

Rissa stiffened when she felt the moist cloth, then remembered their earlier explanation that it was not only their responsibility, but also their pleasure to care for her. And while it seemed embarrassing to have him washing her so intimately, she didn't want to insult him by pulling away or insisting she could do it herself. Mitch was relieved when she simply tried to relax and enjoy being coddled.

RISSA COULD FEEL the air around her shifting and knew Mitch had moved so that he was lying beside her, and she couldn't help but smile to herself. They were so sure she wouldn't know who was where if she couldn't see them, but she had already learned the differences in their touches and scents. As Mitch rolled her onto his chest, he whispered in her ear.

"So, our sweet sub still knows who's touching her, hmmm? Well, we'll have to figure out some creative ways to limit your sensory perceptions of such things when we start playing in earnest." When he felt her tense, he continued, "I'm just teasing you, baby, don't worry. Actually, I'm glad you are so in tune with us, you know us apart by our touch and scent already. That just proves you truly do belong to us." His hands were slowly tracing up and back down her back, almost like a sensual massage intended to ignite rather than relax. "Get up on your knees, baby, and put your sweet pussy over my cock. Ride me."

Rissa was eager to be on top, and as she sheathed herself on his sex, she marveled she could literally feel his pulse beating inside her channel. As she began sliding up and back, she could feel him grow impossibly larger with each stroke.

"Oh God, it feels so amazing this way. You are so deep inside me... oh my God!"

Just as Mitch knew she was getting close to the point of no return, he reached up and drew her shoulders toward him, flattening her against his chest and stilling her frantic movements.

"Shhh, hold still, baby. Bryant has a surprise for you." Just then, Rissa felt the drizzle of lube sliding down the crack of her ass, then a finger rim her hole.

"Oh God, what's he doing? I don't know about this. I don't think I want to do this. Please don't do this..." Even to her own ears, Rissa sounded panic stricken.

Mitch's soft voice filled her ear, "Quiet now, he's only starting to stretch those tender tissues. We won't fuck you together until we know you are well prepared. While a pinch of pain can bring great pleasure, we would never want to truly harm you, and torn rectal tissues wouldn't be anybody's idea of pleasure."

Rissa was listening, she really was, but everything was starting to swirl together in a lust-filled haze. Even though she could still hear his voice and feel his breath against her ear, she was starting to feel like she was floating, and before she even realized what she was doing, she found herself pressing back against Bryant's probing fingers, trying to get him farther inside.

"Stay still, sweetness, I'll get there," Bryant chuckled softly. "You'll have plenty of time for pressing that sweet ass back into us. But for now, I just want to make sure you are good and ready for the small gift we bought for you." She knew she should answer, but all she could do was moan in pleasure. "Actually, it's the first in a series of gifts. Are you curious, love?"

"Ohhh... it feels soooo gooooood... oh, yes... oh, please... series?" Rissa knew she wasn't really making any sense, but mercy, how was a girl to think with Mitch's hot cock pulsing inside her pussy and Bryant toying with her ass? *Oh Lord... I had no idea there were so many nerve endings back there. No wonder the women all rave about being ass fucked by their Doms...*

At Mitch's quick nod, Bryant started to push in the smallest of the butt plugs they'd bought for her. While it wasn't nearly as big as either of their cocks, as a virgin to anal play, Bryant was sure she was going to feel like he was shoving a missile up her ass, and with Mitch buried in her pussy, it would feel even tighter. With her ass basically sticking up in the air, she was completely exposed to him, and as he watched her arousal dripping from around Mitch, the more Bryant worked to coax her tight rosebud to open up to the well-lubed plug. He could hear her starting to pant out her breaths, but she wasn't exhibiting any signs of being in pain or overwhelmed, so he pushed and retreated, fucking her ass with small strokes, gaining a bit of ground with each pass until he was finally able to seat it fully.

"Good girl, sweetness. God, you look so hot. I can hardly wait until we're ready to fuck you at the same time. We'll give you the most amazing orgasms you can imagine."

Mitch had grabbed her hips and was starting to move in and out of her again, and he felt her quickly spiraling out of control.

"Don't you come yet, baby. You need to wait for me, I want to go over that ledge with you." Mitch knew he was going to be right with her, but if she could just delay her orgasm for a few seconds, it would be all that much sweeter for her.

After a few more strokes, he felt lightning race up and then back down his spine before it exploded in a burst of white heat in his balls. The sensation triggered his release, making his cock jerk and his seed shoot so deeply into her cervix, he was certain it would instantly send her over into sweet release, and it did. She erupted in a flurry of muscle contractions that gripped him so tightly, they were just this side of painful.

Rissa screamed, and he wondered if she realized the animalistic sound had actually come from her. He hoped she was experiencing the same light show behind her eyelids he was seeing because they were the most brilliant colors he'd ever seen. The only recognizable thought he had was there weren't any words that came close to describing what he'd just felt. When he knew she thought she couldn't possibly take any more, Mitch shifted his angle fractionally and hit her G-spot, and she was hit by another huge wave of pleasure. He saw her eyes widen briefly before they drifted closed, and he knew her world had faded to black.

Chapter 11

MITCH WAS SURE he had died and gone to heaven. Hell, he'd started having sex when he was fifteen, and he'd never had an experience that even remotely compared to the feeling of knowing Rissa had passed out on top of him. Christ, he'd almost passed out himself. He smiled up at Bryant with what he knew had to be a grin that shouted this would earn him bragging rights for the next sixty years or so.

"Oh, Jesus, I know that look, you think you're some kind of super stud because you fucked our sweet woman into unconsciousness. But don't forget, I was helping, you are not claiming all the thunder for this storm, my friend." Bryant's words were softened by his grin and laughing eyes.

"Help me get her settled, then I really need to check in with Colt to see what they've been able to learn from the jerks they cuffed and stuffed earlier. I'm glad our guys got to them first, and we don't have all the legal restrictions the deputies would have had to deal with. If they got a bit banged up on the way to the local pokey, well, sometimes those things just can't be helped, know what I mean?" He was almost giddy after the mind-blowing sex and knowing his team had secured the intruders.

Bryant was helping tuck blankets in around Rissa, so

she wouldn't get chilled when he asked, "Are you going to try to go in when they're questioned?"

"No, I'm worried about them being a diversion, it was almost too easy. I don't want to risk leaving you two here alone." At Bryant's frown, Mitch rolled his eyes and continued, "Don't give me that look. It's not that I don't think you could or would take care of her, it's just that it's always a strategic error to allow any protection detail to be divided. Remember, even though we both worked for the military, this was more my area of expertise—you build stuff, and I protect it or blow it up." Laughing to himself, he slowly dressed and slipped back into the control room, leaving Bryant to watch over Rissa while he checked in to see how things were going.

KAT HAD BEEN pacing back and forth in her suite until Jenna was sure she was going to wear a hole in the carpet.

"Come on, Kat, sit down. If my Neanderthal brothers know you're doing this—and you and I both know they'll have the cameras on in here—they're going to take my head off for not keeping you calm, and I just don't want to deal with them today. So, give me a break and take a load off." Jenna almost laughed out loud at the affronted expression on Kat's face.

"Are you fucking kidding me, Jenna? Really? You're going to side with them now? After all the years we've been best friends, you want to switch sides? That's just plain mean. I can't even believe you'd add to my anguish... I'm big as a barn, I waddle, I'm bored, I have a case of cabin fever that has me ready to jump the next flight out of

Denver and lie on a beach looking like the whale that I am for the next couple of months. Hell, at least then I could get some cute cabana boy to deliver me virgin drinks with little umbrellas in them. I'd order fruity concoctions, but I'd give them funky names that would allow me to at least pretend they were real drinks. I might even hire someone with a forklift to help me in and out of a hammock close to the water…" Sighing, she plopped down on the sofa and swung her swollen feet up on to the low table holding her orange juice.

Jenna was about to laugh when she noticed tears in Kat's eyes. "Hey, girlfriend, what's with the waterworks?" She quickly moved to Kat's side and wrapped her in a hug. "Talk to me, Kat… what's this about?"

Sniffling, Kat leaned out of Jenna's hug and looked at her friend. "I am just so tired of being tired all the time. I'm huge! Why? I'm only six months along and look at me! Some women are barely showing by this time…" Her voice broke as she started to cry in earnest. Jenna silently bet her brothers would be coming through the door in less than thirty seconds.

Just as Jenna started to speak, the door of the suite crashed open, and both Alex and Zach rushed to Kat's side. Alex was the first to reach her.

"What's wrong, love? Do you feel all right? Are you ill? We can call Doc Woods and have him on Skype right away, or we can send someone down to get him with a tractor. Talk to us."

Jenna started to laugh, but quickly realized that would just aggravate an already emotionally charged situation, so she just discreetly moved toward the door. As she was leaving, she heard Zach's desperate voice.

"Kitten, what on earth is going on? We were only gone

a few minutes. Did you miss us that much? Alex, we'll have to make sure one of us is with her at all times. This can't be good for her or the babies."

Jenna went stock still. *Oh shit… they weren't going to tell her she was having twins until after her sonogram. Oh, big brother, you've stuck your foot in it now.* Jenna realized too late silence had fallen in the room, and when she took a quick couple of steps to make her escape, Kat's voice sounded loud and clear.

"You freeze your happy ass right there, Jenna Beth." She turned to see her friend's laser sharp focus shift to Alex and then to Zach. "Want to catch me up, Zach? Alex? Jenna? Hmmmm?"

Jenna knew a cluster fuck when she saw one, and her big brothers were so not throwing her under the bus this time.

"I have no idea what Zach is talking about, Kat, but I'd sure be interested in knowing the answer. But I promised Selita I'd help her set up tonight's Tex-Mex buffet… so, I really need to be going." Before Kat could protest, Jenna darted through the door, closing it quickly behind her. Breathing a sigh of relief, she was still chuckling to herself when she met Colt in the hallway.

Colt had heard the conversation on his headset and knew Jenna had just lied to her best friend and then left her brothers to deal with their pregnant wife who had been on an emotional roller coaster almost from the very beginning of her pregnancy. The security team had already placed their bets about multiple births, dates, times, and gender in a grid so sophisticated, it was going to take a supercomputer to figure out the winner.

"Pet, did I just hear you lie to your best friend and sister-in-law?" He wanted to laugh out loud at the way she went instantly pale and took a step back. *Oh yeah, you just handed me a perfect excuse to spank that sweet ass, and my palm has been itching for a week.*

"Um, well, yeah, I guess so, but they always throw me to the wolves, and I didn't want her to be mad at me when they were the ones who made me swear not to tell her. You know they're worried about her blood pressure and all…" Jenna hadn't even realized Colt had backed her up until her back was pressed against the door of the suite they were sharing while the addition they would use as a permanent residence was completed.

"I thought I'd made myself perfectly clear that lying, in any form, was something I would punish you for?" Reaching around her to open the door, he leaned close to her ear and whispered, "I've been itching to feel my palm slapping your bare ass for days, and you just gave me the perfect reason to warm you right up. Oh, pet, you are going to be squirming in your chair at dinner tonight." He backed her through the door and closed it, and when Jenna heard him flip the lock, she felt her pussy liquefy between one breath and the next.

"Strip." Colt's one-word command almost had her coming on the spot. She knew he wasn't really angry with her, this was little more than a great excuse to play, then fuck her senseless. She could hardly get out of her clothes fast enough.

After interrogating the trespassers and discovering they had indeed intended to silence the prosecution's principle witness against them, Colt's team had turned them and their taped confessions over to local deputies. Of course, the confessions had required some creative editing on Grayson's part. They didn't want the statements being thrown out of court just because they'd been encouraged by a couple members of his unit who were well trained in persuasive information-retrieval techniques.

Colt had already briefed Mitch and agreed a few more days at the cabin would give them a chance to make sure these two losers didn't have a back-up plan. No one wanted to bring trouble to ShadowDance mansion or The Club, both had seen plenty in the past few months.

Taking a minute to get his head back in the game, Colt ran his hand down Jenna's back and traced his fingers through the crack of her ass before squeezing the soft globes of her ass cheeks.

"You are so beautiful, pet. I'm going to enjoy seeing my handprints bloom a brilliant shade of red over the tawny skin of your ass and know all through tonight's dinner, you'll be struggling to sit still. I'm going to spank you until you're so close to coming, begging for release, then you're going to pleasure me. If you're a good girl during dinner, I'll take you to The Club and maybe, just maybe I'll let you come after I show you off a bit."

He heard her soft intake of breath and smiled to himself. *Oh, you are going to love what I have planned for you at The Club tonight, and Cort is certainly going to enjoy having you as a decoration on his bar as well.* He'd already planned to display Jenna tonight. Introducing her to exhibitionism had been in the planning stages for a while.

Cort Douglas was The Club's bartender, and he also ran the training program for submissives, so he was perfect as a wingman for tonight's adventure. What Colt hadn't anticipated was Jenna playing so perfectly into his hand.

Clasping his large hand around Jenna's dainty wrist, Colt pulled her toward the window. When he moved the skirted lounge chair she used for reading, she noticed a handle mounted in the floor right in front of a low window. With curtains pulled aside, anyone in the gardens would have a clear view of her. He had to fight back his smile when her pulse beneath his fingers kicked up. The sweet scent of her arousal filled the air, and he was thrilled to know she was responding so perfectly to the idea of being displayed.

"Spread your legs apart and bend over and grasp the handle, pet. That will help you hold yourself steady, but you'll still have to use some of those kick-boxing muscles and balancing skills to keep from falling over." There was no way he'd let her fall, and he was sure she knew it, but they were in a scene, and he knew she wouldn't argue at this point.

Their relationship had fairly well-defined rules as far as the D/s elements were concerned. Jenna knew simply by the tone of his voice when they had slipped into a scene, regardless of where they were, and she was such a natural submissive, it was, for the most part, a quick and easy transition for her.

Colt also had a tremendous amount of respect for his fiancée's intelligence and her strength of character. He'd made both points clear to her repeatedly. When they weren't in a scene, he asked for and respected her opinion on a variety of topics. He welcomed her challenges and questions. He was continually amazed at her insight and how perceptive she was to the subtle nuances he faced as the chief of security for the family mansion, the surrounding acres comprising the ranch, and her brothers' BDSM Club.

As Jenna got into position, Colt moved to the cabinet and pulled out a narrow wooden paddle with holes drilled in to it. He didn't plan to use it for all her strikes, but he'd use it for several at the end of her punishment, so she'd have a few welts that would cause her just the right amount of discomfort during dinner. As soon as she settled into position, he landed the first swat squarely over the fleshiest part of her ass; he knew she hadn't been ready, and when she cried out, he knew he'd surprised her. The swat hadn't been particularly harsh, but it would have felt sharp when she hadn't been expecting it.

"Why are you being punished, pet?"

Jenna took a deep breath before answering, "I lied to Kat about knowing she's having twins, Sir."

Fuck it, she was absolutely perfect. God in heaven, he loved her so much, there were times the reality of the gift of her submission humbled him beyond description.

"Very good, pet. Now, let's get this over with so you can use that sweet mouth to relieve the raging hard-on looking at your bare ass has given your Master." Colt didn't spare her, using his hand to land the next six swats, spreading them out and making sure he didn't hit the same spot twice in succession.

"You're taking your punishment very well, love. I'm well pleased with you. The last three will be with the paddle. I'm going to make sure you have a few raised welts across this luscious ass, so you'll remember this during dinner tonight." He could see she was so wet, it was literally running down the inside of her thighs. He watched her adjust her stance, and her breathing was coming in small gasps as apprehension and anticipation battled in her mind.

He wanted her to move past thinking and just let her mind float to that place where endorphins kicked in and happiness prevailed. He stepped back out of her field of vision, so she'd hear the air swoosh through the holes in the paddle before it landed with a resounding smack. Jenna screamed with the first strike. Colt had known the hickory paddle would sting like a bitch which was why he only planned to give her three swats with this particular implement. She was going to be so close to release by the time he finished; he would only have to blow softly on her clit and she would free-fall into a full-blown orgasm without him even touching her. The next strike landed directly on the crease between her upper thighs and the beginning swells of her ass. This time he suspected her scream was as much from frustration as the bite of pain, but it was her heart-wrenching sobs that nearly broke his control.

"One more, Jenna, this will remind you of the importance of honesty for several days, and hopefully, we won't have to revisit this issue again. As soon as this last strike lands, I want you to turn around and drop to your knees. Place your hands behind your back and open your mouth in readiness for your Master's cock."

Before she could respond, he swung the paddle with precision, landing it so the sting would shoot straight to her already swollen clit. Jenna was already dropping to her knees before her screech had stopped echoing through the room, and just for a minute, Colt thought about how grateful he was that all the suites in the Lamont's mansion were soundproofed. God knew he didn't relish the idea of her brothers breaking down the door and seeing their sister's flaming ass sporting three distinctive horizontal welts.

Oh, Jenna, sitting is going to be torture for you for a few days, and dinner tonight is going to be an event to remember.

Chapter 12

TALKING TO COLT wasn't doing anything to allay Mitch's concerns, hell now he was even more convinced the men they'd caught last night weren't the end of the problem. The team had used a lot of creative interrogation techniques and had gotten some information, but it was unlikely these guys were acting alone. It was, however, very likely whoever they were working for would want to tie up the loose end Rissa represented. Everybody involved in the case was convinced the only reason Rissa had been safe until recently was because she hadn't been on anyone's radar until an incident not long ago ShadowDance involving human trafficking higher-ups that had been working with Cal Robertson.

Katarina Lamont had shot and killed Robertson a few months earlier, but there were supposedly hidden diamonds in her possession even though they'd yet to be found. While it seemed unlikely the cases were connected, Mitch and Colt were reluctant to totally discount the possibility. *Fuck it, stranger shit happens all the time.*

Mitch was using several powerful computer programs to analyze and compare all the details of each case, searching for any link. So far, he hadn't found anything of significance, but he'd told Colt he just couldn't rid himself of the feeling that when it all shook out, they were going to find out the cases were interwoven.

Dylan and Melita Marshall would be back tomorrow, assuming the treacherous mountain roads were clear enough to travel. Having the two former special agents weigh in on the situation was going to be more than helpful. Finally, Mitch asked the question he'd been dying to ask since they'd started talking.

"What happened at the mansion today? I have the feeling we missed something interesting."

Colt started laughing before Mitch had even finished asking, "Jesus, you are one scary bastard, you know that?" Mitch didn't bother to respond, he'd been hearing similar comments his entire life. "Well, to start things off, Zach spilled the beans to Katarina about twins, and Jenna denied knowing about it. She straight-up threw her brothers under the bus."

Mitch just waited because he knew Colt better than anyone, and there was definitely more to this story.

"I got the pleasure of paddling my fiancée's beautiful ass for lying, and I can hardly wait until dinner tonight to see how Zach and Alex fared. I'm pretty sure their little kitten turned into a tigress the minute the suite door closed behind Jenna." Laughing out loud, Colt finally added, "There's never a dull moment around here, that's for damned sure."

"Shit, I always miss the fun stuff. Didn't get to chase down the bad guys, didn't get to see Zach and Alex try to squirm their way out of knowing about the twins... but gotta tell you, I'm having a fine time introducing Rissa to my palm." After Colt stopped laughing, Mitch added, "She's perfect, man. She's everything Bry and I have been looking for. Now, we just have to get her to a place where she can accept it, but we aren't there yet. She's suffering from some fairly serious PTSD symptoms. We're actually considering coming back to the mansion, just so she has access to Kat and Jenna's support. I'm not sure Bry and I can give her everything she needs, and we both agree she would benefit from talking to them."

"Understood and agree, totally. I'll talk to Jenna and set up a Skype chat first; let's see how that goes, then you can make the decision. Right now, the roads leading back here from the cabin aren't safe for travel except by snowmobile. Hell, even then, it would be dicey, and visibility is for shit right now." Colt paused before changing topics.

"Have you explained to Rissa she'll face a public punishment when she returns? Fucking Mistress Rachel is really kicking up a fuss. I swear she is the devil incarnate sometimes. She's demanding to be the one to administer the punishment, saying The Club itself was a victim and none of us will punish Rissa as it 'should be done—severely.' She seems to think no one will be hard enough on her. I swear she smells blood and wants her pound of flesh. This isn't all about punishing Rissa for lying to a DM, this is personal, I can feel it. I just don't know any more than that."

"Fuck it… are Alex and Zach on top of this?" Mitch was about to lose patience with The Club's only Domme. Rachel Sutton was a local bank vice president who most of the locals feared for reasons that eluded Mitch. Sure, she was the daughter of the bank's owner, but damn, the woman was straight-up evil, and everyone knew it, so why the hell was she allowed to just grind people into the dirt?

"Yeah, they are," Colt sighed, "but they're in a bad position on this one as well. The more time that passes, the more time she has to rally the troops, and as you can well imagine, she's not limited by the truth or honor."

"You know, I think I'll take a little stroll through her background. I'm tired of dealing with her nasty assed ways. There has to be something in her past that will be useful. Thanks for the heads up, we'll get back there ASAP. And yes, Rissa is aware she has a public punishment coming. Is the plan still to do this at an off-peak time?" Mitch was already setting a plan into motion on another computer linked to multiple search engines.

"Oh yeah, Alex and Zach have also talked to most of the dungeon monitors, they'll be there and will be able to settle any questions among the membership. Trace said to be sure to tell you he's got your back and if you... and I quote, 'want to take the bitch out,' to call him. So, I'd say he might have helpful information for you." Laughing, he knew that had gotten Mitch's undivided attention. Hell, everybody knew Trace Bartell was a stand-up guy to the bone, and if he said he had information, you could bet it was golden.

"I'll call him as soon as we hang up. Did he ever get a lead on the guy who inherited that place next to his? I didn't get a chance to ask him about it, and I know he wanted to get in touch with the new owners and see if they were interested in selling that old place." Everybody at ShadowDance had the utmost respect for the local rancher and Dom. Trace Bartell was known at The Club as "The Gentle Giant" because of his height and demeanor, but he'd been plagued by troubles starting with the untimely death of his wife.

Colt answered, "Last I heard, the guy was expected up here around Christmas, but Trace wasn't betting either way on whether or not some Harvard-educated city boy wants to brave the mountain trails that lead to the old man's shack. Hell, considering the guy isn't likely accustomed to traveling mountain roads in the winter, it's anybody's guess if he'll even show up. I have to tell you, I hope like hell things turn around for Bartell soon."

Mitch was quiet so long, Colt started to wonder if they'd lost the connection. "I think his time is coming. Well, you know what I mean. He's paid a lot of dues, and he's paid even more forward. Losing his wife to a drunk driver, then not only forgiving the young man who was responsible but taking him in and setting him to rights. Hell, he's even paying the kid's college expenses." Laughing to himself, he added, "So if he says he's got the goods on that bitch Rachel, it'll be worth the call that's for sure. I'll call him ASAP."

"Agreed. Keep me advised." Colt heard Jenna begin to stir in the other room, so he told Mitch to take care and not to worry about getting back until they could all do so safely and signed off.

Leaning back in his chair, Colt steepled his fingers over his chest and started to plan ways to entertain his darling submissive during dinner. *Damn, I can hardly wait until I can watch her squirming on that sore ass, legs spread wide open, soaking wet pussy just begging for my fingers to tempt and torture her until she's just a breath away from coming.* Colt had loved Jenna Lamont for years and could hardly wait until her collaring ceremony.

He understood the importance of marriage, but the commitment those in the lifestyle referred to as collaring was far greater than any marriage certificate. Collaring was a Dom's promise to love, protect, nurture, encourage, and cherish the submissive in his or her care. All the Doms he worked with understood that it required a much deeper level of commitment and was not entered into lightly.

By God you don't hear of anyone running off to Vegas to get drunk and collared!

MITCH PLACED A call to Trace Bartell's cell phone and left a message requesting he either return the call or stop by the cabin when he was out checking cattle. Mitch knew the man would be making the rounds, and since he had a pasture near the cabin, it was likely he'd be close enough to swing by for a face-to-face chat. Having an additional Dom around opened up some other interesting possibilities, too. Since Rissa was going to have to endure a public punishment upon their return, it might be a good idea to start acclimating her to being seen by someone other than himself and Bry.

Everyone liked and respected Trace, so he'd be perfect for the scene Mitch had in mind. He quickly shot off an email with the details to both Bryant's and Trace's email addresses, knowing the message would go directly to their phones. Smiling to himself, he had to resist the urge to rub his hands together like a mad scientist... *I love it when a plan comes together.*

Mitch had closed the door between their on-site control room and the playroom while he talked to Colt, not wanting to disturb Rissa, so he wasn't surprised to find her still resting quietly when he returned. He was however, surprised to find Bryant sitting in a chair just watching her sleep.

"What's wrong? Is she okay?"

Bryant's eyes never left her, but his lips twitched slightly. "Oh, she's way more than okay, she's fucking perfect." He finally looked up at Mitch. "I'm just sitting here watching her sleep, and I can't help but ask myself how we got this lucky? I'd almost given up ever finding her, you know? We'd talked about sharing a woman for years, but I'd begun to wonder if we'd ever find one we were both attracted to and who also responded to both of us. Even though we both embrace D/s relationships, we don't usually go for exactly the same things, so finding all those perfect pieces in one woman is just so humbling."

Mitch knew exactly what his friend was saying. While they both loved D/s in the bedroom, they were very different men outside of that environment, and there was nothing ever physical between them. They'd laughed hundreds of times that they loved each other as brothers and that was the end of it and had told each other many times to keep all touches between them to necessity only.

"Colt is going to set up a Skype session with Jenna and Katarina. Since the weather isn't cooperating, we thought we'd give that a try first. Hopefully, they can lend some insight and help her over the rough patches until we can figure out exactly what we need to do to help. I hate feeling helpless, but this is just too important to risk screwing up." He sighed and said, "I'm going to go get started on something for us to eat. Let's move her out of here. I don't want to send a mixed signals about this room, and this sure wasn't the introduction to the playroom I'd planned."

Bryant slid his arms under Rissa's knees and behind her shoulders and picked her up, cradling her to his broad chest. When she made quiet murmurs of protest, he spoke against her ear, "Shhh, love, I'm just moving you to the living room while we fix you something to eat. You can rest in front of the fire, you'd like that wouldn't you?"

Mitch smiled at the sappy look on his friend's face when she simply snuggled closer to his chest, her slim fingers fisting in his shirt. *God, she is so fucking tiny, it's no wonder the guys call her Tinkerbell.* When Bryant looked up, he was sporting the same loopy grin Mitch knew was plastered on his own mug. *Anybody who thinks we have all the power here are completely fucking clueless. She already owns us.*

Walking down the hall, Mitch felt his phone vibrate in his pocket. Pulling it out to check, he was pleased to see a message from Trace letting him know the rancher would try to stop by just after dark. The Gentle Giant assured Mitch he'd be sure to call when he was getting close and he was looking forward to a little playtime.

You know me, boys... always willing to take one for the team.

Chapter 13

B Y THE TIME they got Rissa settled on the sofa, she was starting to stir, and they were sure she wouldn't be sleeping too much longer. It was already early evening, and the snow had stopped falling, so as long as the wind didn't start blowing, they should all be able to return to the mansion sometime tomorrow. While they all had apartments in Climax, Mitch knew they would likely stay in one of the suites above The Club to avoid extra trips up and down the slick and curvy mountain road.

Mitch had already sent word to Alex to have Selita send him a supply list and they'd pick everything up for her on the way in tomorrow. There wasn't much any of them wouldn't do for the pint-sized dynamo who had managed the Lamont household for many years. She kept everyone well fed and didn't hesitate to kick ass and take names when she thought anyone was getting "too fat for their pants." Selita's habit of butchering American slang was a running joke and a great source of entertainment as it become a competition to see who could decipher what she'd meant first.

After setting the casserole in the oven and throwing together a salad, Mitch opened a bottle of wine and left it on the counter to breathe. When he turned to Bryant, he saw him reading his messages and saw the slow smile spread across his face.

"Oh yeah, this will be damn fun and you're right, we need to get her ready for our return. I'm not sure we'll get there early enough to get the punishment done before that bitch and her merry band of miscreants show up tomorrow night, but we need to be ready for whatever shit she has stirred up."

"I hope like hell Trace can give me something to use on that bitch. I'm tired of her terrorizing everyone she comes into contact with. Christ almighty, she's a fucking menace, and the fact that she is targeting our woman just straight up pisses me off." Mitch was pacing in the kitchen by the time he finished talking. He was wound for sound, and he was going to have to work off some of that emotion before laying a hand on Rissa. No Dom worth his salt ever entered into a scene with a sub unless they had their emotions firmly in check; it wasn't smart and more importantly, it was never safe.

"Who's targeting me now?" Rissa's soft voice brought both men's focus to the doorway immediately. Both snapped their attention to the sleep-rumpled pixie, standing idly in the open doorway, looking absolutely adorable wrapped in the soft throw they'd covered her in. Her sleep-lidded eyes and her hair in a riot of soft red curls framing her face before tumbling past her shoulders made her look perfectly fuckable.

"Well, good evening, starshine, glad you joined us. Come here." Bryant held out his hand to her and smiled as she stepped forward, her bare feet making her look even younger than they knew she was. She was a submissive through and through, she hadn't even hesitated to follow Bryant's command. Pulling her to his chest, Bry wrapped his arms around her slim shoulders, and Mitch watched his friend bury his nose in her hair, breathing in the fresh scent of her shampoo. "Oh, love, you smell so wonderful, fresh citrus and lush woman. Perfect." He released her and moved her toward Mitch.

"Come here, baby. I need to hold you for a bit." Mitch's tone was soft, but he could see the underlying truth of his statement didn't escape Rissa's notice. She wrapped her arms around his waist and hugged him back, sensing his need to be held. Listening as her thoughts tumbled from one topic to the next, Mitch smiled at her realization Bryant was more of an alpha Dom. She instinctively knew Bry's demands would always be more intense and his punishments harsher.

He was relieved to know there was a part of her that craved Bryant's strength. She felt Mitch was a softer touch, a trait she attributed to his empathetic gifts, and she was right. His heart clenched at her sympathetic response. Hearing her contemplate how difficult it would be to be continually bombarded by the feelings of others warmed him from the inside. It was rare for anyone to acknowledge what an enormous energy drain it was. He was stunned when she decided he'd need extra love and attention from her, and her commitment to make sure he knew he could always count on her sealed her fate. *Mine!*

"God, you are the most amazing woman in the entire world." Mitch's voice caught in his throat, he'd heard her observations, and she had read him so accurately it had caught him totally off guard. "You are right, baby, it is an energy drain, but over the years I've learned how to shield myself from a lot of it. Right now, I'm frustrated with Mistress Rachel from The Club. She seems to be rallying support to be the one to administer your punishment for lying to a dungeon monitor because she doesn't feel Alex or Zach will do it severely enough." He felt her stiffen and begin shaking in his arms. He'd known she was afraid of Rachel, fuck, every sub at The Club was terrified of the old hag, but he wasn't going to hold back the truth from her either.

"Oh God, she is evil. She'll hurt me. I mean really, *really* hurt me." Mitch could feel Rissa falling into a panic and knew he needed to get the emotion shut down before it completely steamrolled her. Pulling back enough to allow him to look into her eyes, Mitch was pleased to see Bryant step up beside him.

"*Stop!*" Bryant's sharp tone startled Rissa into taking a deep breath and focusing on the men in front of her. "We are handling this, love. You are not to worry about it. This is one of the perks of being a sub, you get to let these types of things go and know your Doms will do exactly the right thing for you. This is going to be a trust test for you, sweetness. Are you going to pass?" Bryant raised a brow and waited.

"Oh, my… okay, well, I guess I can see that… so, well…" Rissa was obviously still worried, but in her heart, she knew none of the men at ShadowDance would ever really hurt her, and she also knew they weren't going to step aside while that evil bitch whipped her like she did the male subs she sunk her vicious claws into.

Rissa had no doubt seen the way she treated her subs, and no one at The Club was surprised when she couldn't keep one longer than a few weeks. Mitch smiled when she finally realized they were waiting for her answer.

"Yes, I trust you. I know you'll protect me and make sure I'm not hurt by her. I know I have to do the punishment, and I'm not as afraid of the pain because I know none of you will take it beyond what I can endure—but, well, I'm really scared of the public part of it. I'm just… well, I'm afraid of all those eyes on me, you know?" Rissa had dropped her gaze to her feet, her fear and insecurity almost broke Mitch's heart.

"Baby, tell Master Bryant exactly why you are worried about the other Dungeon Monitors seeing you naked. I'm cautioning you to be honest because I've already heard it from your clever thoughts—wrong though they may be, those feelings are still very real, and we need to address that right now." Mitch's voice was soft, but steel-edged. He wanted her to verbalize her fears because that was the first step in overcoming them.

Rissa's whole body shuddered, and when she looked up at Bryant, she had big tears in her eyes. "I'm sorry, I know you don't want me to feel embarrassed about my body, but you have to remember, I've had years of hearing people snicker behind my back, and I have these new scars… and…" Slowly, the tears spilled over and were sliding down her deeply blushing cheeks.

Bryant knew there was a time to punish a sub for not loving what a Dom considered his property, and there was a time to love the woman who was struggling on multiple levels with everything she'd been dealing with for the past couple of years. Pulling her into his embrace, Bryant ran his hand in slow circles over her back until he felt her melt into him.

"Now, I want you to stop and think, love. No, don't get all tense, I'm not going to punish you for this although I certainly could—and will in the future. Right now, I want you to stop and consider what about this conversation is contrary to where we want you to be?" Bryant gently moved Rissa back so that both he and Mitch could see her sweet face. He watched her chew nervously on her bottom lip as she thought about his question.

"I think you don't like me criticizing what you consider yours." Her voice was whisper soft, and she wouldn't meet their eyes. After she'd spoken that simple sentence, she was literally holding her breath. Mitch looked at Bry and narrowed his eyes.

"Baby, I have a couple of issues with what you just said. First of all, *what we consider ours*? No, babe, you *are* ours, and you'll do well to remember that from this point forward. Second, this is a discussion and as such, you need to be open and honest. Look at us when you are answering a question, it's a matter of showing respect for us and for yourself." Mitch placed his fingers under her chin and raised her face, so they could study her expression. The tears in her eyes brought them both up short.

"Whoever told you that you were anything less than perfection did you a huge disservice, baby. We're going to make sure you understand that as quickly and with as much passion as we can, do you understand?" Mitch smiled at her when she slowly nodded her head, and he saw her take a deep, shuddering breath, trying to rein in her rioting emotions.

"Very good, love," Bryant said, bringing their beautiful sub's attention back to him. "Now, one of the first lessons we want to make sure you've mastered is this beautiful body is a joy for us to look at. Rest assured there will be times, probably many times, we'll be sharing it with others." Rissa immediately started to hyperventilate and was backing up so quickly, she fell over the ottoman that was behind her. Bryant barely managed to grab her around the waist before she hit the floor. The minute he set her on her feet again, she turned and ran for the door. Bryant couldn't believe she was actually running from them, what the fuck was this about? He hadn't even finished his sentence, and she had gone into full-fledged, fight-or-flight mode, and damn, she was fast on her feet. She was almost to the front door when Mitch caught her easily.

"Clarissa, stop right now and tell us what you heard that made you run. And for Christ's sake, woman, look at the way you are *not* dressed... How long would you last out in that snow?" He easily scooped her up and brought her back to the sofa. Settling her on his lap, he placed his hands on either side of her face and turned her to face him.

"Talk to me, baby, because there has been some huge misunderstanding for you to react that way to what Bryant hadn't even finished explaining to you." Like lightning her thoughts raced through his mind. "Oh... sweetheart... never, never, ever against your will. The bastards who kidnapped you talked about sharing didn't they?" He didn't wait for her to answer. "Oh, baby, we had no idea those are the words they'd said to you." When she started shaking all over, he held her tightly, whispering sweet words of comfort against her hair.

Bryant took her from Mitch and settled her on his lap. "Remember, you have a safe word, and we'll be checking with you even more in the beginning to make sure you're always at green. If you aren't, it's your responsibility to be honest and let us know. You can't depend on Master Mitch's special gifts because strong emotions often wipe out what he can hear. It's on *you* to speak up... understand, love?"

When Rissa didn't answer right away, Bryant put his hands firmly on each side of her face to help her focus solely on his words. "Baby, that was a direct question, you must always answer every direct question quickly and honestly." When she nodded her head, he added, "And

115

with words. These same rules will be in effect at Shadow-Dance. It's a good idea for you to follow them from the beginning. Remember… we begin as we intend to go."

"Yes, Sir, I understand. I'm sorry for trying to run from you. I have no idea how I thought I could outrun either of you. I just panicked." Pushing her hand through her tangled curls, she shook her head. "I wonder sometimes… will I ever get over these crazy fears? There have been so many different times I thought I was going insane."

Both men assured her she wasn't insane, and that they were certain both Katarina and Jenna would be able to offer valuable and healing insight if she would just open up and talk with them. She agreed to try and was just settling down when Mitch's phone rang. When he saw Trace Bartell's name displayed on the screen, he smiled and moved out of the room as he quickly answered the call. After a short conversation, he was back and nodded to Bryant.

"Baby, we're going to have company in a few minutes. We want you to get accustomed to being seen and touched by others before we return to The Club tomorrow. Master Trace is also stopping by because he has some information about Mistress Rachel he believes will be helpful in getting her to back off what has become nothing but a glorified witch hunt against you." Rissa's eyes widened, and Mitch felt her struggle to identify which part of that information was causing her the most concern.

Rissa knew Trace Bartell, so she wasn't afraid of him. She'd heard him referred to as "The Gentle Giant" by her spa patrons because he was just under six and a half feet tall but had a relaxed, easygoing air about him women and men alike gravitated toward. Since his wife's death a while back, he'd taken in the young man who had been drinking and caused the accident that claimed her life. He'd set the troubled teen on the right path before he ended up in the state's correctional system. From what Rissa had heard, the kid was now in college, his education being funded by Bartell's huge ranching operation. Everyone expected the kid to meet his goal of becoming a veterinarian and someday returning to the ranch to work.

"Witch hunt? Oh my… can you tell me exactly what you mean by that?" Rissa's voice was shaking, and even Bryant could feel the anxiety coming off her in waves.

"I mean she seems hell-bent on making sure she gets to whip you during the busiest time at The Club in full view of all the members. That's not what Alex and Zach have planned, but she is trying to stir up support among the members, and since so many locals are concerned about the financial lever she holds over them, they're grudgingly supporting her."

Rissa wasn't moving, hell she was barely breathing.

"Now, baby, don't panic. You know the Lamonts aren't going to fold on this, and they will always do the right thing. It doesn't matter what pressure she puts on them, but it does stand to have a significant impact on your business as well as theirs."

"Oh shit, I hadn't even considered that. I can't take a financial hit like that… God, I'm just barely getting by now, and Alex and Zach aren't even charging me rent for my space." She had started biting her bottom lip again and stood quickly pacing the width of the room. Even though they should have settled her down, she was so cute pacing back and forth in front of the fire, they simply enjoyed the view for a few minutes.

They'd allowed her to put on one of Bryant's white dress shirts, so it was a pleasure to sit back admiring the view of her luscious body being outlined by the firelight. It was certainly no hardship to wait while she attempted to sort through some of the emotions flooding her. The shirt hung nearly to her knees, but when backlit by the fire it was completely translucent and highlighted every soft curve. Her breasts bounced and swayed perfectly as she stalked from one side of the room to the other, the tight muscles of her ass flexing below the gentle curve of her slender back. Her legs made up the lion's share of her petite stature. Mitch and Bryant were both smiling like fools before she finally turned to look at them, completely puzzled.

"What? Why are you both giving me that silly grin?"

"Well, love, that's quite the peep show you're giving up each time you pass in front of the fire, and we're just enjoying the view." Bryant tried, but failed to keep the amusement out of his voice.

"Oh shit! I didn't realize... oh my, I'd better get upstairs and get dressed. How long until he arrives? Do I need to make you all something to drink? How about cookies or a cake? Oh dear, what about dinner? I'll bet he hasn't eaten dinner, either, I'd better make sure we have enough for him as well." She was fluttering about like a pretty butterfly that couldn't decide where to land first because all the flowers seemed to be demanding her attention.

"Baby, calm down. Dinner is taken care of, it's in the oven and will be ready by the time we finish talking to our guest. We've already set out wine and made the salad. You can thank Selita for the wonderful meals when we return to ShadowDance. She always keeps our freezer well stocked." Mitch smiled as he saw her relax. He heard her mentally planning to go upstairs to dress for dinner and smiled to himself. *Not so fast, sweet cheeks. You are already overdressed for what we have planned.*

Bryant didn't need Mitch's gift to know what their beautiful little sub was thinking. "No, love, you are not changing a single thing about what you're wearing, except to unbutton that last button and let the shirt fall open. Remember, your beautiful body belongs to us, and we're planning to show it off a bit this evening after our chat and dinner." He had to bite the insides of his cheek as her mouth dropped open in surprise. "We also want you to get used to kneeling when our guests are present. Now, come over here and let me show you exactly what we'll expect of you."

Mitch moved to the front door while Bryant helped get Rissa into the position they preferred for their subs. Helping her to kneel down on a small rug, so her ass cheeks rested on heels, Bryant pushed her knees wide apart, so her pussy was perfectly displayed.

"Put your hands behind your back and hold them loosely one in the other so your breasts are lifted and presented like the gift they are for our viewing pleasure and touch." He also explained she should keep her eyes down unless told to raise them by a Dom who was directly addressing her. With a quick kiss to the top of her head, he stood back and sucked in a breath at the beautiful view. *Holy fuck, she's so gorgeous like this, she takes my breath away.*

Just then Mitch returned from answering the door with Trace Bartell in tow. Mitch smiled and nodded.

"I couldn't agree more, my friend, our little sub is breathtaking." Turning to Trace, he asked "What do you think, Master Trace?" He watched Trace smile when Rissa tensed. Her mind might be fighting it, but her body was definitely on board, judging by the glistening juices coating her sweet pussy lips and her tightly peaked nipples.

"Well, I can't think of any better greeting. She is stunning. Her posture is exactly right, and her body is as close to perfection as I've ever seen." Mitch had filled him in briefly on the challenges they'd been facing with her, so it seemed Trace was determined to hit the high points right away and put her a bit more at ease. He moved to circle her slowly before kneeling in front of her and placing his fingers under her chin. "Look at me, little one."

Rissa raised her eyes to him slowly, but at his warm expression, she finally let out the breath she'd been holding. Trace did nothing but smile at her for several long seconds before continuing.

"You are truly a vision, and these two had better thank God above each and every single day for the gift of your submission. You make sure you keep them in line, okay?"

It took a few seconds for Rissa to realize he'd actually asked her a direct question. "Y–yes, Sir," she answered softly.

"Now, if it's okay with your Masters, I'd like you to sit on the sofa while we talk." At their nods, Trace placed his hands on her slim shoulders and lifted her as he stood up. "I have some information that's going to be very valuable for you even though I'm afraid some of it may come as a bit of a shock as well." He watched her expression closely for any fear and was pleased when he didn't see anything but warm affection and relief. "Now, let's get something to drink and we'll sit down and get comfortable, so I can give you the dirt on Rachel Sutton."

Chapter 14

A s THEY SAT relaxing after a wonderful dinner, com-
pliments of Selita, Trace leaned forward with his
arms resting on his knees. "I have to tell you… that was a
damned fine dinner. I've tried to lure Selita away from the
Lamonts so many times, it's a wonder they haven't banned
me from ShadowDance." His words were softened by his
light expression and low, rumbling chuckle. "Damn, maybe
I should just marry her?" He asked more in jest, but Rissa
was touched by the note of melancholy she heard in his
tone. Before she realized what she was doing, she'd
reached over and squeezed his hand.

"You'll find a woman who will bring joy into your life
again, you just wait and see. And when you do, she's going
to be one lucky lady." She smiled at him, then realizing that
she'd touched a Dom without permission, she froze,
worrying she had overstepped her boundaries.

Mitch reached over, laying his hand gently on her
shoulder. "Baby, no one is ever going to complain about
you being kind to someone. Please don't get so caught up
in the rules of D/s relationships that you let them change
who you are. We love you just the way you are. Don't
change that kind heart of yours, ever." His words were like
pure sunlight shining into her soul, and she could practically feel their healing effect seeping through her. "We have

no desire to change you or control you. Dominance and submission are for sex and play—none of us are into a 24/7 slave lifestyle."

Glancing at all three of the men, Rissa felt like they had lifted a huge weight off her shoulders. She didn't really understand why because this wasn't any different from what they'd said before, but something about it just seemed to sink into her soul this time.

"You know, Rissa, sometimes we have to hear things several times before we believe them," Trace chuckled. "I know I'm like that, and thank you, I appreciate your kind words more than I can say." He took a couple seconds to compose himself before speaking again. "Grief is a strange thing, you think you've worked through it, and then it blindsides you again. I've been blessed beyond measure by good friends who have been there for me every step of the way. In some ways, I understand what you are going through—you think you're ahead of this thing, then something sends you reeling, doesn't it, darlin'?"

"Oh yes, that's exactly it, and I don't ever see it coming. It's so hard to explain to someone on the outside." She squeezed his hand again. "Thank you for understanding. And I meant what I said too, the woman you choose is going to be very blessed to have you in her life." Rissa leaned back in her chair and wanting to lighten the moment and change the subject, she added, "Now, please tell us what you know about Hagatha." Her broad grin brought laughter from all three men, and Trace looked particularly relieved with the change of topic.

"Well, first of all, I want to tell you the funny thing, just because I can, and I've kept her nasty little secret far too long." The expression on Trace's face was one of pure mischievous boy. "When Rachel was in college on the west coast, she was the girlfriend and submissive of a rather famous porn star, anybody remember the name Johnny Dong?" His grin spread ear to ear at the men's chuckle. Rissa didn't seem to recognize the name and that didn't surprise any of the men; it was likely her exposure to extreme BDSM media was limited, at best. "Well, they were quite an item for a couple of years, her old man was fit to be tied, let me tell you." They all shared a laugh thinking about old man Sutton's reaction to his daughter running in those circles.

Bryant had grown up locally as well, but he was a couple of years younger than Trace. "Were you two classmates?" he asked their guest.

"Yes, but the big deal was our parents were very close friends. Her old man was a terror, I'm telling you. Hell, the old fart is still hell on wheels, literally… those nurses out at the Good Samaritan Center draw straws to see who is going to have to deal with him." When they all laughed, he added, "I remember him showing up at our house one night after midnight. I'd been up half the night with heifers that were calving, and I was completely exhausted. Anyway, he shows up with a damned plane ticket and instructions on what hospital Rachel was in. He wanted me to go get her and drive her home. Damn, I had too much on my plate, but he wouldn't take no for an answer. My old man stepped in and said if Sutton would pay for two men to replace me, then he would go along with it. Well, long story short, I flew out to California, rented a car, picked up a badly battered Rachel Sutton, and drove her back here."

"Why you?" Rissa remembered Rachel moving back to Climax when she herself had been in high school, but she hadn't known all the drama surrounding her return.

Rubbing his face, obviously remembering a less-than-pleasant memory, Trace continued, "Old man Sutton had always wanted Rachel and me to end up together." He shuddered, honest to God shuddered; Rissa couldn't help but laugh at his reaction. "Oh, go ahead and laugh at my predicament, little one, but remember, we haven't had playtime yet." Flashing her a warm smile that told her he was enjoying the lighthearted teasing, he went on.

"Oh, he'd been pushing that particular agenda for years. It wasn't ever going to happen—she and I had *both* told him that many times. We were barely even friends, let alone interested in becoming lovers. But I have to tell you, after she moved home, she was different. She would never have been called a sweet girl to begin with, but she returned here a harsh woman. And believe me, her old man made her pay dearly for her transgressions. Anyway, that's only part of her story, but it lays the groundwork for the rest." Trace had paused for a long moment, then leaned back and gave Rissa a considering moment before speaking directly to her.

"Rissa, what do you know about your maternal grandfather?"

The question caught Rissa totally off guard, and she was sure her expression showed her surprise at the turn the discussion had taken.

"Well, not much really, I know Granny always said he left right after she found out she was pregnant with my mom, and she never married again. Why? What does this have to do with Rachel Sutton?" Rissa had always questioned her Granny's story, but she'd never mentioned those doubts to anyone else.

"WELL, LET ME ask you this… was Doc Woods around a lot when you were a kid?" Again, Rissa was surprised by his question. "Rachel's issue with you has very little to do with the incident at The Club, that's just her excuse; her real motive is money—a whole lot of money." He was looking right at Rissa as if he was searching her expression for any hint of deceit, finding nothing but confusion he continued.

"Darlin', your granny was a wonderful woman, everyone in town loved her dearly, I want you to know that." Trace saw the trepidation beginning to cloud her eyes. God, he hated being the one to tell her this, but it couldn't be helped, so he'd just as well get it over with. Leaning forward and grasping her small hands in his large, calloused ones, he continued, "Your granny and old Doc Woods had a long-term love affair. He was married at the time, but he and his wife had been living apart for several years when your granny became pregnant with your mama. Doc tried to get his wife to agree to a divorce, but she wouldn't hear of it. His wife was old man Sutton's sister, Elizabeth."

Rissa sprang to her feet, breaking free of his hands so suddenly, he hadn't had time to react. She started pacing furiously, back and forth in front of the fireplace again. They could hear bits and pieces of her self-talk, but not enough to be able to figure out anything she was saying. She finally stopped in front of Trace.

"But how does this involve money? I don't understand this at all."

Trace moved to the sofa and grabbed Rissa's wrist as she stalked by. Pulling her front and center, he sat her on the coffee table in front of him, looking straight into her beautiful green eyes.

"Elizabeth Sutton-Woods died of a drug overdose when you were a tiny baby. Up until that time, Doc had to keep his relationship with your grandmother and the fact he was the father of her child quiet or at least, as quiet as you can keep anything in a small town."

He chuckled and continued, "It was common knowledge he loved your grandmother deeply, and that he financially supported her, so she could devote as much time to raising your mama and later, you as she needed. Now, all that being said, with your mom being in the wind, you are legally his only heir." When her eyes widened, and she started to shake her head, he said, "Yes, it's true. But if you weren't around to claim it, it would fall to her. It's my understanding his will is written that the money can only be inherited by an heir who has lived continually within a fifty-mile radius of Climax for two years prior to Doc's death." Personally, Trace thought the restriction was insane. In his view, you simply left your estate to the person you wanted to have it and kept all ridiculous restrictions out of the mix.

RISSA WAS GLAD she was sitting down, she was sure her knees wouldn't have held her. Her mind was reeling with all the information she'd been given.

"You see, little one, if she can get you to move by shaming you publicly—and don't bother to deny it, I can tell by your expression it's crossed your mind—she stands to inherit millions in not only cash assets, but it also seems our local doctor is a hell of an investment wizard as well, so his stock portfolio is huge. Not to mention the old fart also owns real estate all over the damned country."

Laughing to himself, Trace thought about all the times he'd tried to get the old coot to sell him some land he owned bordering the Bartell Ranch, but the old goat wouldn't even talk about it. Instead, he insisted on continuing to rent it to Trace at the same price Trace's dad had paid five decades ago. Doc didn't need the money, and that was the end of it as far as he was concerned.

Mitch leaned forward and took Rissa's small hand in his much larger one, damn, but her fingers were like ice. He gently pulled her over and lifted her onto his lap, wrapping her in the warmth of his embrace.

"Baby, tell us what you're thinking."

Honestly, Rissa didn't even know where to begin, she was so stunned. Everything she'd always thought she knew about her family had just been turned on its ear. She had no reason to doubt Trace, but it was almost more than she could absorb at one time.

"I-I don't even know where to begin—I'm just, I don't know, really. I guess I'm just kind of in shock, and it's going to take me a while to process this all, you know?" Looking up at Trace, she said, "Thank you for telling me, I know it wasn't easy for you. But if nothing else, it gives me a chance to get to know Doc as the grandfather I always wished he was, well, is… geez, this is all so confusing."

Mitch continued to rub her back in quieting motions but looked at both men and knew they were all thinking the same thing. Time for a bit of distraction. If they left Rissa to her own thoughts, she'd work herself up into a real state.

"Well, baby, I want to take your mind off this for a

while. I understand you need time to work through this, but for now, we're going to play a bit." He had turned her to face him, and when he saw her eyes dilate quickly, he knew he'd made the right call.

Trace watched as the pulse at the base of Rissa's slender neck sped up quickly, her breathing coming in shallow pants. He was thrilled for his friends. She was beautiful, and her immediate reaction was telling.

"Oh, little one, I can see the change in your breathing and pulse from over here. And I'll bet if one of your Masters runs his fingers through your sweet pussy, they'd find you soaking wet and ready for them already. Am I right?"

Rissa was falling into a lust-induced haze quickly, so her reaction time was slowing, and it took her several seconds to realize she'd been asked a question. "Yes, Sir, you're right." She might have agreed, but that mean she understood how she could be thinking about sex now, but she was.

Bryant sensed she was baffled by her own response. "Love, sometimes it's easier to switch rails and head in a different direction when our train of thought is getting all bogged down." At her puzzled look, he added, "In other words, sometimes you just need to give your mind a break. Your body is usually more than willing to go along with the change that's why it reacts so quickly to sexual stimuli even though it seems like your brain is trailing behind." He finally felt like he was getting through when her cheeks blushed a lovely shade of pink.

Bryant was behind her, so he leaned over her shoulder and spoke to their guest. "Master Trace is in the perfect spot to check out his observation, and I'm going to ask him to let us know what he finds." Nodding to Trace, he watched as Rissa's head leaned toward the sound of his voice, and he heard her moan softly as Trace reached under the shirt she was *almost* wearing. Bryant was already sporting a monster erection, but when he saw how wet Trace's fingers were when he pulled his hand from beneath the shirt's hem, it got worse. Watching the rancher suck the glistening arousal from his fingers pushed even closer to the edge.

"Oh, she tastes just as sweet as you said she would. You two are lucky bastards for sure." Trace loved women, and he genuinely liked Rissa. He wanted to help her heal from what had to have been a horrific experience. She had made herself "one of his" just by reaching out to him earlier, that small gesture of kindness had assured he would always look out for the little bit of woman all the Shadow-Dance regulars affectionately called Tink.

She was well-liked by the staff as well as The Club's membership, and God only knew how tough that crowd was to please. If you weren't genuine, everybody knew it the minute you crossed the threshold. And while he was thrilled for Mitch and Bryant, there was still just a twinge of jealousy lurking beneath the surface, not that he'd ever let it show. Though she was a tiny little slip of a woman, there was a core of strength there, and he admired the hell out of that above all else.

Mitch slowly turned Rissa so her back was against his chest and directed her to hook her dainty feet on the outsides of his calves. When he spread his legs, he parted hers even more. With sure fingers, he reached up and pulled the placket of her shirt apart, sliding the soft cotton garment far enough off her shoulders, he could use the long sleeves to tie her arms behind her back. While she could have easily wiggled her way free, the restraint was mostly mental, and with a sub like Rissa, every bit as effective as the heaviest chain.

Bryant moved, so he was leaning against the mantle, watching intently. Trace was still sitting, but his body was practically vibrating with energy and need. Bartell was a great Dom and a devoted mentor at The Club. Mitch hoped he found a woman soon; it was a shame to see someone who would be so great with a sub spend so much time working to avoid the loneliness at home.

TRACE DIDN'T MOVE a muscle, but Rissa sensed the change in him immediately. Gone was the affable gentleman whose company she had enjoyed at dinner. In his place was a Master, a Dom who was very much in control. It had always amazed her how The Club's Doms seemed to morph into different people right before her eyes. It had been spooky the first few times, but for the most part, she just accepted it as her "new normal" as she liked to refer to the lifestyle differences associated with her D/s infatuation.

Rissa instinctively knew she needed to stay still and wait for instructions. This was not the time to be self-directed. She had to bite the insides of her mouth to keep from smiling. *Damn it, Rissa Jean, you know better than to think, just let it go and feel. I'm telling you if you smile, you're gonna find yourself ass deep in alligators right here in the Colorado Rockies.*

Mitch was struggling to not laugh out loud, damn, but she was a hoot to listen to. "Baby, you are right about it being best to stop thinking, but I have to say, we really need to chat about your little self-talks. And I'm sure

Masters Bryant and Trace would love to hear all about those Rocky Mountain alligators later on. But right now, I think Master Trace would like to play with your sweet pussy and see just how responsive you are. Now, I want to warn you, you aren't allowed to speak or come without permission. Do you, understand?"

Trace had already moved to kneel in front of her and was sliding his fingers through her wet folds even as she was answering.

"Oh my God, oh my God, oh my God." Her voice was already breathy, she wasn't going to last five minutes if Trace made any effort at all, and he would because the entire purpose of this was to make sure she earned a small punishment. They wanted to get her used to having another man's hands not only giving her pleasure, but also a bit of punishment. This evening was all about getting her ready for what she would experience tomorrow. The better prepared she was, the less likely it was to trigger a flashback.

"Little one, I don't believe that is a proper answer." Trace lightly slapped her directly on the pussy, causing her to gasp in surprise. He smiled, knowing it had to have stung, but he was certain it hadn't truly hurt. The surprise was meant to bring her attention back to what she'd been asked—damn, but she was amazingly responsive. She was so wet with arousal, it was literally dripping out of her channel. "Better try again. Do you understand that you aren't allowed to speak or come until one of us gives you permission?"

Rissa's head had fallen back on Mitch's shoulder, but she raised it to look at Trace with half-lidded eyes. "Y–yes, Sir." She finally managed to answer, but Trace would bet the bank it had been rote memory and hadn't involved one single decision-making brain cell. Bryant chuckled softly behind him, and Mitch's grin confirmed that they were in agreement.

Trace held up two fingers behind his back to Bryant, indicating he'd make her come in two minutes or less, then he started working his fingers in and out of Rissa's vagina, teasing her swollen clit, circling it but never giving her exactly what she wanted. In thirty seconds, she was moaning and thrashing her head back and forth. She kept trying to push her hips forward, but Mitch had a strong arm wrapped around her waist to keep her anchored in his lap.

With his finger slick with her juices, Trace slid it from where it had been circling her clit, moving to the opening of her channel before sliding along her perineum until he could draw lazy circles around her ass. Reversing the path, when he reached her clit, he circled it twice before giving it a firm squeeze. He knew the move was guaranteed to send her over the edge, and she didn't disappoint him. She screamed, and he watched her cum shoot over his hand and groaned at the pure eroticism of the moment. *Jesus, Joseph, and Mary, she is amazing. If I can find a woman half as lovely and responsive as this one, I'll thank God each and every day for his gift.*

Trace looked up to see her eyelids sliding down slowly as she floated back to earth.

"Oh, little one, I'm pretty sure that was an orgasm. What do you think your Masters are going to have to say about that?" He was struggling to keep from laughing at her horrified expression. The poor girl, she'd been set up to fail. He *almost* felt bad.

Bryant stepped up in front of Rissa and crossed his arms over his chest. "Love, I do believe you have earned a punishment. While I do love watching you when you're lost in release, you had not been given permission to do so." Rissa shuddered and looked up at him through her lashes, and he could clearly see her expression wasn't one of fear but rather sadness. She was obviously upset she had let them down. And even though he wanted to pull her in to his arms and reassure her that she was never a disappointment, this was about preparing her as much as possible for tomorrow's public display, so he just held her gaze for a few seconds before continuing.

"Since you came with Master Trace's fingers sliding through that wet pussy, he'll administer his swats to your bare ass first, using his choice of implement. I'll be second, and I'll be using a leather paddle. Master Mitch will be last and will make his choice at that time." Bryant wanted Mitch to go last as he knew Rissa better than either he or Trace and would be better able to determine where she was at that point.

Mitch helped Rissa stand up and moved her into position by having her stand with her feet slightly more than shoulder width apart bent her over, so her hands grasped the edges of the coffee table. Trace stepped up behind her first and rubbed his palms slowly over the globes of her ass.

"You have a beautiful ass, little one, all ripe and round, just waiting for my palm to turn it a glorious shade of deep pink. I'll be using my hand for your punishment today because I want to make sure you are properly warmed up for your Masters who will follow."

He gave her a few seconds for the anticipation and anxiety to reach just the right levels; the perfect balance between the two was essential for any submissive's punishment, but it would be critical in Rissa's case. He said, "Remember, no coming," just as his palm hit dead center on both cheeks.

Rissa gave a small squeal more from surprise than pain, and when he held his palm over the place he'd struck, she felt the burn seep all the way in until the fire reached out to touch her pussy from the inside. She felt more than heard herself moan as he raised his hand and smacked her harder this time right on the crease between her upper thigh and her butt cheek. Again, he held his hand there for a lingering moment, making sure she felt the full effect of the strike.

The next swat was in the same spot but on the other side. She suddenly realized, she was getting wet again. When he gave her the last two swats in quick succession, she felt her juices rush down the insides of her thighs. *Oh craptastic, this is just about the most embarrassing thing ever. Damn, I hope they don't notice that.* Oh, hell no, her luck was not that good... ever.

Running his fingers through her sex, Mitch said, "Damn, babe, I'm starting to wonder if this is really going to be much of a punishment at all, seems you enjoyed Master Trace's palm being planted on that sweet ass of yours. You are soaking wet. After Master Bryant and I are finished, we'll see if we can all relieve some of that pent-up need pouring off you in waves."

Rissa felt herself being readjusted a bit and saw Bryant step up with a leather-covered paddle.

"This is brand new, love. It will never touch another woman's ass. Like Master Mitch and I, it now belongs only to you." He smacked her dead center the first time, and it was solid, but not hard enough to make her scream.

The next two swats hit each cheek and were so close in time, she had barely registered the first one before the second landed. Immediately, he was rubbing her ass, making sure he wasn't going to leave lasting marks or bruises. He didn't mind her being uncomfortable sitting for the next few hours, but they didn't want to push her beyond what they felt was tolerable. Sliding his fingers through her wetness and circling the dark pink rosette of her ass, Bryant pushed the tip of his finger in just enough to cause her to moan and thrust back into his touch.

"That's right, love, push back against my fingers, show your Master how much you want him there. We'll give you what you need in just a bit, but for now, feel that little bite of pain, just a slight burn to match your ass."

He continued to fuck her ass with his fingers, barely deep enough to ignite a burning need before removing them and landing two more swats. These two strikes had more force behind them, causing Rissa to gasp and rock up on to her toes. Bryant smiled in satisfaction. Rissa was perfect. She enjoyed the edge of pain, the telltale gush of her sweet nectar down her legs all the reassurance Bryant needed to know he hadn't given her more than she could handle. She was enjoying this punishment, so tomorrow was going to be easier for her than they'd hoped.

Mitch had been listening to her giving herself a pep talk at the beginning, then he'd enjoyed her wandering thoughts as she tried to understand how the pain could make her feel so needy. Before Bryant had finished, she was teetering on the edge of orgasm, so Mitch was going to give her a minute to cool back down, *literally*.

Reaching over to a small glass of ice he'd left beside his chair earlier, he pulled out a small cube that had been rounded slightly by melting and reached between her thighs.

"Don't move, baby, I need to cool you off a bit. Remember, if you come again without permission, we'll have to start all over again, and I, for one, would rather get on to the fucking part of tonight's activities."

His chuckle would reassure her he wasn't angry, and that helped her stay in position. *Holy crap on a cracker that is so damned cold on my pussy. Wish he'd rub that ice up on my flaming ass where it would be useful.* Mitch was glad she couldn't see his face because he nearly snorted out a laugh as he listened to her. Damn, but he loved her with everything in him. She was amazing in so many ways, and he wanted to learn one new thing each day for the rest of his life—and if he lived to be one hundred and twenty-four, he just might have learned everything wonderful there was about this sweet woman.

"Now that you are a bit more grounded, baby, I'm going to use my belt on your ass. I wanted my implement to be something I wear close to my body, and this is a wonderful leather. It'll be perfect for putting five nice stripes across this beautiful, lush ass." He'd no more than finished speaking, then the first strike landed at the very top of her ass. He knew it sent a streak of fire zinging through her system like lightning.

Oh, my fucking God that hurt so bad, I'll never survive four more of... Before she could even complete the thought, the next two landed in short order working their way down her ass. She was sure her ass was on fire. *Yep, the smoke detectors will start screeching any second, you just wait and see.*

The next strike was over that crease they'd each hit, but the belt set it completely on fire. She was sure she'd have blisters when this was done. He moved up closer to her, and before she could register he was leaning over her from a different direction, she felt the tip of his leather belt connect with her pussy lips just as Bryant spoke in to her ear.

"Come now, love. Let us hear your pleasure."

She let out a scream and started to shake from the inside, feeling the waves of orgasm race toward her fingers and toes from her core. She collapsed, but Trace had been ready and caught her easily around the waist. She felt like she was having convulsions, but she couldn't control it, she didn't think she was ever going to stop coming.

Mitch had known she was dancing on the edge, but her reaction stunned him. He'd never had a woman react to a punishment at his hand so strongly. He found himself wafting between pride in her, pride in himself as a Dom, and wonder at the gift God had given him as the desire to bury his cock deep inside her raged through him like a primal urge strong enough to break him in half.

"Damn, baby, that was fucking amazing." He knew she was so lost in the moment, she probably hadn't even registered he'd spoken to her, let alone understood the words.

Trace picked her up and stood her in front of her Masters, but he kept his hands on her waist, making sure her knees didn't go out from under her again. He leaned over her shoulder and spoke close to her ear.

"Well done, little one. You took your punishment with an amazing amount of grace and dignity. I'm proud of you as I know your Masters are as well. Now, kneel and thank them for the lesson." He helped her kneel and stepped back.

From her position in front of both Bryant and Mitch, she spoke softly. "I'm so sorry I let you down by coming when you hadn't given me permission, Masters. Please forgive me." She knew she'd been set up, but she also understood their plan had come from a place of love and compassion. It was obvious they were trying to get her ready for what was to come, and they wanted to minimize the chances she might be flung headlong into the terror of a flashback and embarrass them and herself.

"Oh no, baby, we aren't afraid you'll embarrass us, we just didn't want you to have to endure any more trauma if it could be avoided." Mitch reached forward and pushed her soft curls away from her heart-shaped face.

THE PLAN HAD been for Trace to participate in the sex, but the moment felt too intimate between these partners. He'd been slowly backing away from them when it occurred to him Rissa would take it as a personal rejection, so he walked back up to her. Sensing his plan, both Bryant and Mitch stepped back. Trace stopped in front of Rissa, looking down at her tenderly. He could only hope his eyes would convey the warmth and respect he felt for the little sub.

"Little one, you are amazing…" He saw immediately the doubt cloud her eyes. "And I will gladly join your Masters in reminding you of that anytime they see fit to invite me. But right now, this moment is about the three of you. I'm leaving, but believe me, it isn't because I don't want to be here for the rewards." Smiling down at her, he said, "I'll be there tomorrow and any other time you need me, do you understand?" When big tears filled her beautiful green eyes and spilled over, he used his thumbs to wipe them away.

"There are many people who will be in your corner tomorrow. I want you to remember that. I'll intervene with Mistress Sutton before she makes her way to you— what was it you called her? Oh yes, Hagatha. Damn, I like it—I believe I'll use that among some of the younger Doms tomorrow and watch it catch in the wind and spread like wildfire."

Chuckling, he placed a kiss on her forehead and whispered in her ear. "You have a second chance you know. This is it, grab it with both hands, darlin', and don't you dare let go because every single day with those you love is a gift." With another quick kiss to the top of her head, he turned and quickly made his way to the door.

Mitch thanked him for his help before showing him out. Turning back, he didn't waste any time catching up with Bryant who was carrying their woman down the hall to the master bedroom. They had big plans for their little sub tonight, and he couldn't wait to sink into her sweetness. But first they'd attend to her and make sure she was back on level ground, and… then, all bets were off.

Chapter 15

THE DRIVE BACK to ShadowDance the next morning was treacherous even though the roads had been cleared the afternoon before. Strong winds overnight had drifted the narrow mountain roads shut in several places, forcing Mitch to blow through the drifts faster than he would have ordinarily traveled in such conditions, particularly with such precious cargo.

Rissa sat ramrod straight in the front seat between both men and stared straight ahead. She'd donned sunglasses because the bright sun reflecting off the pristine snow would lead to snow-blindness quickly without adequate protection. Bryant had been texting with the staff at The Club and knew things were set up and would take place immediately upon their return. No one saw any benefit to making Rissa wait until later in the afternoon to get this punishment put behind her. She was already nearing her saturation point of anxiety, and everyone agreed getting this over with as quickly as possible was in her best interest.

As they pulled up to the front steps of the Shadow-Dance Club, Rissa started to hyperventilate. Mitch was physically exhausted from the strain of the drive and was relieved when Bryant took her hands and forced her to breathe with him in a slow three count until she had settled enough they could get her inside The Club. As soon as they entered, they checked in, turned to Rissa, and had her give them her coat and shoes.

Sally, one of ShadowDance's regular subs, was standing to the side, ready to take Rissa to the locker room to change into the outfit they'd arranged to have ready for her. Bryant turned her to face him, holding both her trembling hands in his larger ones.

"Now, love, you'll go with Sally to the locker room and change. Sally has all our instructions, and she'll see to it you are properly attired before she returns you to Alex and Zach's office. They want to talk to you before we all head downstairs, do you understand?"

Bryant wanted to take her in his arms and whisk her away more than he had ever wanted anything in his whole life. If he could have changed anything, it would be reporting to other Club staff that the pint-sized sub had lied to him when making her escape from The Club several weeks ago. Hell, in many ways he felt he was just as culpable because he had gotten distracted and basically, let her walk away without even challenging her story. But wishing certainly wasn't going to change a thing, so it was best to get this over with and move on.

Rissa nodded her head, but at Bryant's raised eyebrow, she said, "Yes, Sir" so softly, he might not have heard her if he hadn't been looking right at her.

Patting her firmly on the ass as he turned her toward Sally, he reminded the other sub, "Remember, exactly as instructed or you'll be right up there with her, understood, Sally?"

The other woman looked at the floor and spoke out clearly, "Yes, Master Bryant, we'll follow your instructions to the letter and return to the office immediately." At his nod, Sally took Rissa by the elbow and quickly led her down the hall. They hadn't got far when Bryant heard Sally say, "Come on, girlfriend, I'm going to help you get all dolled up, and you're going to show this place what a class act you are… you hear me? I want to see some of that spunk I know is in there. You can do this… you can rock this, girl!"

Bryant looked at Mitch and smiled. "God love Sally. Remind me to send her a big gift basket full of the girly shit I know she loves but won't buy for herself."

Mitch laughed, and knowing Sally was a single mom who was taking college classes on-line along with her full-time job working at The Club as their Housekeeping Manager, suggested.

"Maybe we could get her some gift cards for takeout food, textbooks, and child care? Those are the things she really needs, but I agree, adding in some spa products would be a nice touch. I'll ask Jenna to help us; God knows, she'll love getting to spend some of our money." Laughing, he turned to follow Bryant to Alex and Zach's office.

ALEX WAS SITTING behind the massive oak desk with his feet propped up and his chair leaned back, but his relaxed pose was in sharp contrast to the anger Zach could feel brewing just below his twin's cool exterior. Zach was pacing the full length of the room, eating up the distance with giant strides, all the while muttering obscenities directed at that bitch Hagatha. Zach wasn't exactly sure where that nickname he'd heard a younger Dom use a few minutes ago had come from, but it suited Rachel Sutton to a fucking tee as far as he was concerned.

After gesturing for Mitch and Bryant to take the seats across from his desk, Alex looked at both men and cursed under his breath before speaking.

"God damn it to hell, I fucking hate this. I no more want to punish Rissa than I want to sleep out in the damned snow... again! But Rissa has put us in a piss poor position, and Rachel Sutton is standing to the side, swinging a damned noose." Alex's voice was ice cold, and while Mitch had served in the Special Forces with both him and Zach and had heard that exact tone before, Bryant was taken aback by the obvious fury waiting to erupt.

Zach stepped forward then and shook both men's hands, welcoming them home. "I don't know exactly what Trace Bartell's role in this is, but he pulled that bitch into one of the private rooms a few minutes ago. He was carrying a large envelope and wouldn't say anything except we weren't to start until he had returned, and we were not to use any electronic monitoring in the room while they were in there. Do you two have any idea what this shit is about?" Zach stared at them both and was shocked to his toes when both Bryant and Mitch broke out in huge grins.

"Oh yeah, we spent some quality time with Trace last night, and he told us about this plan, but honestly, guys, it's his and Rissa's story to tell." At his boss's raised brows, Mitch added, "I swear to you on the lives of our team, this is pure fucking gold." Just then there was a quiet knock on the door.

Alex bellowed, "Come," and winced at his own harsh tone when he saw a wide-eyed Sally and a totally terrified Rissa enter the room. Alex watched as Sally reached over and grabbed Rissa's hand and gave it a quick squeeze. Alex felt like an ass, knowing he'd made it necessary for Sally to reassure Rissa she'd be safe in their care.

"My apologizes, ladies, I didn't mean to shout at you. It isn't you I am annoyed with, and I want to make sure you know my mama would be mighty pissed off if she'd heard that." He smiled and could see Rissa's muscles relax, and she finally seemed to have taken a breath.

Rissa had always been amazed at how Alex Lamont's smile seemed to totally transform his looks. While he and Zach were mirror-image twins, Alex was usually the more somber of the two, but when he smiled, the effect was devastating. Zach had always been the more easygoing of her bosses, but he could go completely Dom on you in a New York minute as well. They were both alpha through and through, and Rissa had wondered many times how tiny little Kat Lamont handled them with what appeared to be an amazing amount of ease.

Zach stepped up and said, "Sally, take a minute to powwow with your friend here, give her your last-minute pep talk, then be on your way downstairs. You are not to be in the Main Lounge, but make sure you are close by if we need you." Reaching over and placing his large hand on her shoulder, he gave it a squeeze. "We owe you one, sweetheart, and we'll make it worth your time being here, I promise you."

"Yes, Sir, and thank you for your offer, but I'm here because it's important to my friend. Rissa needs to know she knows she has friends… a lot of friends who care." Sally had looked directly at Zach, something she rarely did as a Club sub, but his admiration for her had just gone up like a Titan missile. *You are worth your weight in gold, sweetie, and the four of us are going to enjoy making sure Cort stops dicking around and claims you as his own very soon.* The Club's bartender and sub trainer had been dancing around his attraction for this sweet sub long enough. It was time to push his ass into the game. No more standing on the sidelines whining about wishing he could play ball with the big boys. It was time for Cort Douglas to step up.

Sally stepped right in front of Rissa, and putting her hands on the smaller woman's shoulders, spoke clearly enough for everyone in the room to hear.

"You go out there, and you show everybody exactly how much strength it takes to submit. You show them you are a kick-ass chick, you hear me? Your fear is your *only* enemy in that room and don't you forget it. And when this is done, we're gonna have ourselves a margarita movie night and hack up Hagatha with word hatchets all night long!" Sally gave Rissa a blinding grin and pulled her in to a crushing hug before stepping back and walking with her head held high out of the room.

Rissa looked up at the four men watching her, taking a deep breath, waiting for their instruction. All four men were speechless for a few minutes, bowled over by Sally's words and Rissa's bravery in the face of her obvious fear. Bryant finally recovered and held out his hand to Rissa, and she immediately moved to him.

"Love, we are waiting for Master Trace to finish talking with Mistress Rachel. We aren't expecting him to be long, but he has asked that we not start without him. As he told you last evening, he wants to make sure he was in the room to provide you with moral support."

Mitch waited for a sign Rissa was tracking the conversation and not slipping off into fear, and when she nodded and said, "I understand, thank you for explaining, Sir," he nearly burst with pride at her response.

"Now, perhaps while we're waiting, you might have something to say to Masters Alex and Zach?" He knew she felt terrible for letting down the men who had given her a job and a chance to own her own business when she had first returned to Climax. She'd been drowning in her recovery, sitting all day and night alone in her little studio apartment above a bar downtown and had almost given up reclaiming her life when they'd stepped up. They'd not only offered her a job, they'd also provided her with a custom-built spa right inside The Club itself. Bryant watched her eyes go bright with unshed tears, and her nod was all the answer he needed.

Moving to stand in front of them, Rissa kept her eyes downcast but spoke clearly.

"I want to apologize to you both." Nodding to each of them, she continued, "Master Alex and Master Zach, you have been so kind and generous to me, and my horrible display of disrespect for not only you both but each and every one of The Club's Dungeon Monitors shames me more than I can begin to tell you. I've earned this punishment, and I'll try to accept it with quiet grace and dignity, so you will know the depth of my desire to begin rebuilding your trust and faith in me." She let out a shuddering breath and small wonder, hell, there wasn't a one of the men in the room who had taken a breath the entire time she had been speaking. Alex and Zach were stunned speechless at the sincerity and humble spirit of her apology.

Alex stepped forward and took her hand in his and tilted her chin up, so she met his gaze. "You are amazing. I am sure neither of us has ever had to punish someone when we wanted it any less than we do at this moment. While the rules demand a public punishment, they do not specify what that punishment must be." Zach stepped forward and took her other hand and continued.

"Our sweet wife and our not-as-sweet sister,"—they both laughed—"poured over the rules and assured us that while it says we both must be present, we don't have to mete out the punishment." Zach looked up and saw it was starting to dawn on Mitch and Bryant exactly what they were saying. "We decided how this was handled was dependent on how you presented yourself during this private apology to us. And, sweetie, that was the most honest and sincere apology I've ever heard, and you make us proud to be your friends and bosses."

They both stepped back and pulled her by the hands over to her two Masters and placed her hands in theirs. Alex looked at them and grinned ear to ear.

"You are welcome to use any punishment you see fit, but I personally have found delayed gratification to be quite effective with Katarina."

Zach's laugh echoed around the room before he added, "Oh yeah, that seems to wire her up like an eight-day clock. As soon as Trace gets here—" Before he could finish, Trace knocked and walked into the room, smiling like the cat that had swallowed the canary. "Well, speak of the devil…"

"The devil, am I? Well, I'll have you know there is a woman storming out to her car at this very moment who would be in full agreement with that assessment." He looked like he was about ready to burst, wanting to share what had happened, but he was also relishing the moment. "Oh, and before I forget, here's her membership card." He dropped a handful of torn pieces of paper on the desk. "Seems she isn't planning to use it any longer, but here it is, just the same."

Rissa's eyes had gotten wider each time Trace spoke, but when she saw the shredded card, she looked up at Trace, and big tears filled her eyes.

I have the best friends in the whole world. God above, I don't know what I did to deserve these people in my life, but I'm going to thank you each and every day from here on out, I swear it.

Mitch smiled down at his sweet sub, and said, "I think Master Trace has earned a hug. He's gone to bat for you today, baby, and he came out swinging like the loyal friend he is."

Rissa's quick nod was followed by her short sprint toward Trace, and when she launched herself the last few feet, he caught her easily in a tight hug. She spoke in between her soft sobs.

"You are the best, Master Trace. I am blessed to have you as a friend. Thank you from the bottom of my heart."

Trace laughed and ran his hands over her now very much exposed bare ass and said, "Oh I'm really enjoying this heartfelt thank you and the feel of your very bare bottom, little one."

Rissa gasped and started trying to pull the super short dress down over her ass even as her face lit up in a brilliant crimson blush. God, how had she forgotten the crazy thing Mitch and Bryant had left for her to wear was little more than wide strips of very short fabric sewn to a ribbon band that was held just barely over her nipples by thin ribbons over her shoulders.

When she'd first seen it, she was sure it had at one time been a very short sundress that someone had cut into strips, but Sally has assured her it was made like this for a good reason… total access.

Mitch had known exactly what would happen when she went to hug Trace and had thought this would break the ice a bit and help get things moving in the right direction. Alex and Zach's news and suggestion for a punishment changed what everyone had been dreading like death into something they would all be able to remember fondly and laugh about over drinks for many years to come.

Bryant stepped forward and grabbed her elbow. "Come along, love. I believe we have a punishment to deliver and an audience waiting for us in the Main Lounge." Rissa took a deep breath and was suddenly filled with anticipation instead of dread. Oh, they were still going to punish her, and she was sure they were going to push her to her last thread of control, but now, she was looking forward to showing everyone just how devoted she was to both of her Masters and how much she trusted them to give her just exactly what she needed. She was ready to take that first step out over the edge, knowing in her heart, they would be right there to catch her.

Chapter 16

RISSA STRETCHED AND rolled over, feeling the smooth texture of silk sheet caressing her naked body. In her half-awake state, she was dreaming of water softly flowing over her and the sun warming up the water around her as she lay back, basking in the afterglow of amazing sex. Just thinking the word "sex" brought her more fully awake as the memories of last night's "punishment" came more into her mind's focus.

How could anything that was supposed to be painful feel so amazingly good? That was a mystery she planned to bask in and wonder about... later. Yes, she'd think about that later, right now, all she cared about was stretching her tight muscles and enjoying the slide show of pictures from last night playing through her mind.

Mitch and Bryant had tied her to the St. Andrew's cross that had been set up on the small stage at the center of the Main Lounge at The ShadowDance Club. They'd used a butterfly over her clit to wind her up to the point she'd been begging for release within the first five minutes. The soft leather strips of the pussy flogger brought the blood to the surface, so that her labia literally throbbed with each beat of her heart.

Her Masters had worked together to bring her to the edge of orgasm so many times, she'd lost count. The other

Dungeon Masters had watched with rapt attention until they'd known her Masters were finally going to bring her to completion, then quietly slipped out, giving them privacy while she screamed her Masters' names as they fucked her together for the first time. They'd promised her it was going to give her an orgasm like none other, and they'd delivered… big time. Rissa had been afraid she was going to shatter in a million pieces and evaporate into a fine mist from the heat of their fucking. It had been beyond anything she had ever imagined could even exist.

Coming back to the present, she rolled over to gaze out the window looking down into what was known as the gardens that lay between ShadowDance and the mansion. She marveled at the Winter Wonderland spread out before her. Sunshine made the snow sparkle as if a million diamonds had been scattered atop the trees and shrubs. Jenna's wedding was planned for just a few weeks from now, and construction crews were hard at work fulfilling every wish and command of the Lamont family matriarch, Catherine Lamont.

Rissa admired everything about Alex, Zach, and Jenna's mother—she was gorgeous, brilliant, kind, and orchestrated workers like a five-star general. Smiling to herself, she remembered how she had watched in awe as Catherine had single-handedly made sure the bridge over the creek running behind the house and the gazebo positioned in the center of the bridge had been completed in time for her sons' wedding to Katarina McKay.

Everyone had sworn it couldn't be done, but she and Bryant had worked together to design it, despite him being on the other side of the globe. No one was willing to tell Catherine Lamont that her plan was impossible to complete. Rissa loved that Catherine not only always looked like she'd stepped out of a fashion magazine—owing to her career as a model before her marriage—but she was also no stranger to hard work.

Catherine Lamont believed in living by example and practiced her motto of "Don't ask anyone to do work you are not willing to do yourself" by showing up at the bridge site on several occasions in boots and jeans and did whatever job the foreman asked of her. She'd had every man on that crew eating out of the palm of her hand in less than an hour.

Rissa watched as Catherine made her way down the snow-covered pathway to what was affectionately known as "The Garage." The staff had gone together and purchased a large neon sign with those words in bright blue because the lead mechanic was a fan of all things 1960s. The entire garage crew had spent most of Christmas afternoon installing their gift in a workshop that was every bit as sophisticated as the shop in any big city car dealership. The female members of the Lamont's staff loved having on-site mechanical help that kept their cars in tip-top shape as a "benefit" of their employment. Rissa had no doubt Catherine was planning to make a trip into town, undeterred by the dangers of driving on the slick mountain switchbacks. Chuckling as she saw Catherine's husband Daniel sauntering along behind his wife, she laughed out loud when she saw Daniel stop his love with a word. Watching from above, Rissa could see their discussion playing out below and knew while Daniel didn't exert his dominance over his sweet wife very often, it was always simmering just below the surface. When it didn't appear she was being convinced, he leaned over, placed his shoulder in her midsection, and simply picked her up and began making his way toward The Club's back entrance.

Rissa could see Catherine's laughing face, her eyes fairly dancing with joy as they disappeared in to The Club. Only then did Rissa become aware of Bryant standing alongside the bed, watching her intently.

"It's amazing, isn't it? They have been married for almost forty years, and they still love to play. I'm not sure I have ever known a love story quite like theirs. Someday, ask Alex or Zach to share it with you, their parents' story is really quite remarkable." He sat down on the bed and was gently drawing his fingers through her tangled curls as he let the silence stretch out, seemingly lost in the moment.

Rissa loved these moments of quiet connection, she craved the intimacy as much as any other aspect of her relationship with Mitch and Bryant. The feeling of belonging to them and the ShadowDance family was humbling and a blessing she'd never expected to find.

"What are you thinking, love? You look sad all the sudden." Bryant's voice was pitched with concern, and she knew he'd watched the emotions flit across her beautiful face.

"No, I'm not sad, really. I just understand how lucky they are to have each other, you know? I have always envied that in couples I'd see together, no matter their ages. Sex is amazing… I mean you and Mitch have shown me just how incredible it can be." She ducked her head with a shy smile when his eyes flashed with barely leashed passion. "But it's the intimacy that's even more important to me, that feeling of belonging. When you grow up being moved around by a mother who just kind of floated between jobs and men before being left with your grandmother in the middle of the night, you understand the value of that level of commitment. It humbles and awes me to watch it."

Bryant was stunned by her words and for just a moment, couldn't manage to speak around the lump that had formed in his throat.

"Oh, love, you are so perfect. Your heart is open and huge, your soul is pure light, and your body responds to Mitch and me in ways that are so far above anything we'd ever hoped to find, it's still almost more than we can believe. Mitch and I will spend the rest of our lives giving you exactly what you just watched out that window."

"What did she see out the window?" Mitch came into the room and immediately settled down alongside Rissa. "Good morning, sunshine, or I guess I should say good afternoon." Mitch leaned over and kissed her temple before turning his attention back to Bryant. "Now, what was so interesting about the Lamonts?"

Rissa started to giggle, and before long it was a full hold-your-stomach, tears-rolling-down-the-cheeks laugh before she said, "Leave it to our resident empath to only get a bit of it before he—"

She didn't even get to finish the sentence before Mitch had rolled her on to her back and was straddling her. He pinned both her wrists together with one hand, raising them over her head between one heartbeat and the next.

"Now, baby, you really might want to think carefully about that taunting thing when dealing with your Doms. Because I have to tell you, I can be pretty wicked and creative with electronic gadgets, and I have several that are almost ready to be used on that sweet pussy and ass of yours." His voice was all business, but his expression was brimming with mischief.

"And that's supposed to frighten me—Sir?" She tried to hide her amusement and was sure she had failed miserably.

"Well, Master Bryant, I think our little sub is looking

for trouble. What do you say we take her up on that challenge this evening? We can reserve a room at The Club, or we could just play in one of the public lounges, what do you think?"

"Hmmmm, tough call. I say we do a bit of planning this afternoon and surprise her." Bryant had known Mitch was going to try to arrange to have the evening off. They had big plans for their little sub and couldn't wait to set things in motion. "Since tomorrow is Thanksgiving, there should be a good-sized crowd at The Club tonight. I can hardly wait to show off our little princess here." He leaned over and gave her a scorching kiss before they both got up off the bed and stood with arms crossed over their chests and watched as her eyes widened, and she gasped even as her nipples became stiff points, and they could smell her arousal.

"What? That's it? You get me all… well, all…"

"All what, baby?" Mitch's amused tone didn't do a thing for her good humor… Nope, not one single thing even remotely close to satisfying about that. She was completely exasperated now.

"Oh, crap on a cracker, you know what I mean. You got me all hot, and now you're just going to walk away? Well, you'll see, I don't need you to take care of this." She knew she was skating on very thin ice and waving the threat of self-satisfaction in front of a Dom was like waving a red flag in front of a bull, but she just couldn't seem to stop the words from tumbling out. "Oh yeah, I got along for years before you two came along, and as long as they still make batteries, I'll be able to do just fine on my own."

She didn't even see them move, they were that fast— she was up and bent over the edge of the bed before she had even blinked. The first two swats landed hard, and

Rissa gasped at the sudden fire spreading over her skin. The next three were harsher with the last one landing directly over her pussy.

"Shit! That hurts! What the fuck is wrong with you two?"

Bryant growled, honest to God, growled. "Watch your language, and your taunting just went way over the edge, pet. You know your pleasure belongs to Master Mitch and myself. You will not touch yourself with the intent of providing self-stimulation unless directed to do so by one of us—are we crystal clear on this point?"

Rissa was in full-on pissed-off mode now. "Crystal clear, indeed... *Sir!*" She probably should have made an effort to keep the sarcasm out of her voice, but she didn't and until the next several swats landed on her already-blistering ass cheeks, she hadn't cared. But now? Damn, sitting was not going to be much fun for a while, that was for sure. She was pissed, and she didn't really even understand why, but everything was overwhelming her.

It felt like she was being swept away by huge tsunami-strength waves of emotion and each wave was different from the last one, so she couldn't ever get her feet under her. When she was crying and apologizing, they finally stopped the spanking, and it was Mitch who helped her up and sat her on the edge of the bed. Handing her a box of tissues, he tilted her chin up, so she was forced to look at him.

"Baby, you know better than that. You are better than that bratty behavior. If you are needy, tell us. We won't always accommodate you, sometimes because we have something else planned and having you on edge for a while before a scene will serve to enhance your pleasure. But this blatant disrespect for your Doms is demeaning to you as well and will not be tolerated. Do you understand?" Mitch waited patiently for her to agree.

"Y–y–yes, S–s–s–sir." Shuddering with her sobs, she added, "I'm sorry, I don't know why I did that. I knew I was saying all the wrong things… but my mouth wasn't paying any attention to my brain." Rissa only wanted to be alone, she would have told them anything if she'd thought it would get them out of the room sooner. She planned to head down the mountain and hide away in her small apartment above the local tavern and just sleep.

The physical pain hadn't been so much she couldn't stand it, but this had just proved to her she was in way over her head. They wanted to get inside her head, and she wasn't ready to be that open with anyone. Her counselor had told her again and again she was ready but opening up was harder than she'd ever imagined it would be.

She'd worried a thousand and one times if she would ever be able to overcome the PTSD triggers. Even she realized her reactions were inconsistent, and there was no question they'd be noted by two experienced Doms. She needed time to process everything that had happened, and she couldn't do that here at ShadowDance.

Rissa had agreed to the time at the cabin, but since they'd returned to The Club and mansion, there wasn't any reason to continue delaying the inevitable. She could tell when Mitch started picking up her thoughts again. *Thank God strong emotion blocks him temporarily at least.* And she purposely blanked her plans from her mind. He looked at her intently before speaking softly.

"You're learning to block, I don't like it."

Bryant stepped forward. "She's learning to block her thoughts from you? Really? I didn't know that was possible." Reaching over, he cupped the sides of her sweet face and used his thumbs to remove her remaining tears. "I hate having to punish you, I would much prefer the only spankings you get are erotic and meant to bring you pleasure. But I won't ever hesitate to take you in hand if you act out like a spoiled brat." When Rissa didn't answer, he let go of her face. "We'll stop in to check on you later. Get cleaned up, dress, and go downstairs. Make sure you get something to eat. We'll tell Selita to expect you."

After they had both left the room, Rissa hurried to get herself cleaned up, quickly made her way out to the garage and was halfway down the mountain when her cell phone started ringing. Glancing at the screen, she saw Kat's phone number. Hitting the button for speakerphone, she immediately heard Kat's frantic voice.

"Are you okay? Holy shit, I overheard the men talking downstairs, and when I looked for you, I couldn't find you anywhere. I called the garage, and they told me your car wasn't in the lot. Oh damn, girl, you are going to be in deep shit when Mitch and Bryant get wind of this. I bought you some time by telling the garage guys I had forgotten you were going to the store for a few things, but it won't be long before the shit hits the fan. Oh man, I hate being a hippo… I'm missing all the action… we could have escaped together, damn and double damn… I haven't had a good spanking orgasm in so long, I think I'll have forgotten how."

Damn, Rissa loved her bosses' fireball wife. She and Katarina had become good friends over the past few months, and Rissa never tired of Kat's rapid-fire, out-loud thinking. After a few beats of silence, Kat's voice came through the phone in a much softer tone.

"Really, Rissa, are you okay? I'm worried about you. Talk to me, girlfriend."

Rissa wasn't sure she would be able put her feelings of being overwhelmed into words that would make sense even to her sweet friend. She was little more than a bundle of raw nerves, but she took a deep breath and let it out slowly before answering.

"Thank you for checking on me, I'll be fine. I just need some time to process everything. I haven't felt this vulnerable and powerless for a long time, and it's shaken me, you know?" Chuckling to herself, she continued, "Of course, you know. I'm sorry, that was really insensitive of me." She took another steadying breath.

"I'll be all right, I just want to sleep in my own bed covered up by the quilt my Granny made for me and eat a quart of ice cream and a package of cookies." She tried to put laughter in her voice, hoping Kat would be appeased. "That cures everything, right?"

Kat wasn't convinced, but she'd been in Rissa's position and knew when it was time to back off and let a friend work through a rough patch.

"Well, you make sure you keep that phone close. I heard there has been a man in town asking about you, and that mega bitch Rachel Sutton is still on a rampage about you. Watch your back and lock your damned door. *Please*, call me later and let me know you're okay. It's not nice to make a preggo woman worry, you know... bad for the ole high blood pressure."

"All right, mother hen... I'll call you later." Rissa had to laugh, leave it to Kat to pull that card out when it was convenient. "I know the guys will be busy at The Club tonight, so we'll trash talk them and both feel better. Now, I have to go, the road is slick, and my tires are not in the best shape. I need all my attention, or I'll be making car skiing a new sport. And, Kat... thanks... for caring... you are a great friend."

She heard Kat sniff through the connection. *You have to love emotional pregnant friends.* Kat just said, "Right back atcha'. Hugs and call me later." And then she was gone.

Driving down the mountain was treacherous, and more than once, Rissa questioned the wisdom of trying to get back to her cold, bleak apartment in a car that was ill equipped for the snow-packed roads. By the time she pulled in behind the tavern, her usual parking spot was filled, hell the whole block was full. Holiday weekends were always hopping at the little honky-tonk bar. It was a gathering place for everyone in town visiting family and friends. Many of these early patrons would be heading up to ShadowDance later, so at least the noise level would ease up after a while. She finally found a parking place a couple of blocks over and cursed her high-heeled boots with every step on the icy walk.

The wind picked up, so she'd pulled her hood up to cover her ears and shield her face. Rissa was usually acutely aware of her surroundings, being a kidnapping victim had deeply ingrained that cognizance within her. It was telling about her emotional state that she hadn't noticed the couple standing in the shadows, watching her make her way up the back staircase and into her frigid studio apartment.

"I told you she'd come back here, eventually. Now, when are you going to get rid of her?" The woman's voice was shrill and reminded Maks of fingernails being raked down a chalkboard.

"I have already told you, Mr. Petrov is planning to take care of this himself. He is on his way but will not be here until tomorrow. The flights into Denver were booked solid; what the fuck is with all this travel for eating turkey, anyway?" He'd never understood Americans' fascination with a holiday revolving around a bird. But they followed-up with a holiday celebrating a loud, fat man in a strange red suit, so what did he know? He'd grown up in the slums of Moscow, so celebrations of any kind had been little more than government sanctioned events. Holidays were not recognized in his family, because the only thing they had ever respected was money.

"We just needed this visual, I wanted to make sure you had given me the correct information. Your motives for helping us are... what should I say it? Questionable. I don't trust you."

Rachel Sutton was immediately indignant. "What do you mean you don't trust me? You wanted me to let you know if I saw her, and I've delivered. I don't know why you don't just go get her and lock her in the trunk of your car until your boss gets here. You know the men from ShadowDance will be here before morning, don't you?"

"Indeed, we do know, and we are better prepared this time. We have no need for your advice. You will have your reward, and she will be gone. Why is that so important to you anyway?" Maks knew women like this one never did anything without a self-serving motive, and judging by the way she was dressed, she wasn't in desperate need of the paltry sum she was being paid.

When she didn't immediately answer, he wasn't sur-prised and simply said, "I'm going into the bar for a beer. I suggest you get home before someone sees you standing in the alley with a man you aren't going to be able to explain to your society twit friends." He started to walk toward the bar and was pleased to hear her head in the other direction. Perhaps he'd ask around a bit and see if anyone knew just why the bitch calling herself Rachel was so determined to see his target out of the picture. *You can never have too much information—perhaps there is more money to be made from this disaster before Petrov arrives.*

Chapter 17

Rissa made her way through the dark, cold, studio apartment she'd called home since returning to Climax. She'd cleaned out her Granny's house and put it on the market almost immediately after she'd been cleared by the government's evaluation team. How they could rescue you and then hold you for months in what they'd called "Protective Custody" she had never been able to figure out.

The house sold within hours; she'd received an absurd offer so far above the small home's market value, she'd called the realtor to make certain the paperwork she'd received wasn't in error. He had assured her the offer notation was correct as was the stipulation that the seller not be given the buyer's name. While she thought it odd, the money had been such a godsend, she'd signed and promised to have her belongings out by the end of the next week. While she still didn't know who the buyer had been, she did know whoever it was had a heart of gold because she'd been told she could leave her belongings in the house as long as she needed to. She had finally managed to have the house completely cleaned out a couple of months later. The memories of the last time she'd closed the front door and turned the well-worn key in the lock still brought her to tears.

Quickly turning the dial on the old heat register against the large windows facing the street, Rissa looked around at her bleak surroundings and sighed. Exhaustion and emotional overload were taking their toll, and even though she could feel the pounding bass of the dance music below, she was just too frazzled to care. After a fast trip to the bathroom to wash her face and brush her teeth, Rissa returned to the main room and collapsed on the oversized stuffed chair she'd brought from Granny's. Pulling the soft afghan she kept draped on the back over her, she finally let the tears fall. Without another thought to the phone she'd turned off before returning it to her purse, Rissa cried herself to sleep.

MITCH WAS IN a panic by the time he reached the top of the stairs and rounded the corner to the room where they'd left Rissa a few hours earlier. He had gotten tied up with work; reports of a man with a foreign accent asking questions about The Club and Rissa kept him holed up in the Crow's Nest much longer than he'd planned. Bryant had offered to deliver the clothing they planned to have Rissa wear for tonight's Club scene, and when he'd found the room empty, he'd called Mitch.

After several phone calls, including one to the garage, they surmised their woman had panicked and run. *Fuck it all. What a damned novice mistake. We knew the morning was intense, damn it. Leaving her to her own coping devices was not a mistake any experienced Dom should ever make, let alone two of us.* As he made down the long hallway and finally stepped into the room, he came face-to-face with Bryant whose stern expression told him there was something important going on.

"Let's go. We're meeting Alex, Zach, and Katarina in the office." At Mitch's puzzled expression he continued. "Seems Mrs. Lamont has information her husbands have persuaded her to share."

Finally, a small smile crept over Bryant's tight lips causing them to curve upward ever so subtly. "That woman is going to be sitting on a pillow for months if not years with all the punishments she's racking up. I swear, sometimes, I think she is trying to push them into paddling her bare ass now. I think she's bored if you want to know the truth, and she's topping from the bottom in every way she can think of, and they're simply not taking the bait. But they will exact every single punishment after she delivers, I have complete faith in them."

They were almost to the bottom of the stairs when they heard Alex's voice booming from the office.

"Katarina, I love you with my entire heart and soul, but if you don't sit your lovely ass in a chair this very instant, I swear I will not be responsible for my actions." *Oh joy, the boss is already wound for sound.*

Katarina was stalling, plain and simple. He knew it. Zach knew it. And Katarina knew it. What they didn't know was why, but they damned well knew who would be able to find out. From the look on her face when Mitch walked through the door, she also knew exactly how this conversation was going to play out. Alex watched her shoulders sag in defeat. *Good, finally some sign of the submissive we married. God, I don't know if I'm going to survive this woman let alone the babies he could see dancing in her round belly.* Alex and Zach both loved lying beside her, staring at her naked middle, watching as small fists and feet pressed outward as if trying to touch the daddies they heard talking to them from an outside world they couldn't wait to join.

The instant Mitch cleared the door, he sensed his role and moved to sit by Kat. Taking her small hand in his, he opened himself up to listen to her random thoughts.

"Kat, Rissa seems to have gone missing. There are some things happening in town that make it less than safe for her to be alone. Please, tell us anything you can that will help us keep her safe." Mitch had gone straight to her heart, he'd known playing the safety card would be the quickest way to get information. Katarina Lamont had a heart as big as a woman twice her size, and her experience as a victim would make her even more vulnerable to his argument.

Kat gasped at his words but continued to look at him thoughtfully, trying to judge his sincerity and what level of threat he posed to her friend. Alex growled from the other side, "Katarina." His voice was low, and her name drawn out, but the message was clear. She merely held up her hand to him, giving him a clear signal to stop.

"I'm not stupid, Alex, if Rissa's safety is in question, I'll tell you everything, but I want to ask Mitch and Bryant a couple of questions first." Turning her gaze to Bryant she asked, "What is your plan with Rissa? Are you playing or serious? I've seen you very little since your return, and everything I know about the person you are now is secondhand information." Smiling a smile that didn't reach her eyes, she turned to Alex and then Zach. "Not that my husbands would ever mislead me or withhold valuable information or anything you understand—but I'd like to hear this one directly from you if you don't mind." Her comment made no attempt to conceal she was still angry about her husbands not telling her they'd known she was having twins for almost a month before it had been inadvertently revealed during an argument.

Mitch had to suppress a smile. *Oh yeah, I tried to warn you she was going to have your balls on a platter when she found out, but did you listen to me? Fuck no... and you can just stew in it, boys.*

Bryant moved, so he was squatted down directly in front of Kat and took her other hand into his, looking deeply in to her eyes.

"Katarina, I adore Rissa. She is everything Mitch and I ever dreamed of finding in a wife and partner. The love I feel for her touches the very bottom of my heart and sends warmth to parts of me I was afraid would never feel warm again." He hadn't even realized he was caressing the backs of her knuckles with his fingers, and he wondered if the movement was meant to soothe her or himself. "Please help us keep her safe. Did you talk to her before or since she left the mountain?"

Sighing deeply, Kat turned to Mitch. "What about you, Mitch? Tell me you aren't playing with her, she won't be able to survive that, you know? She's just still too fragile. She'll get stronger with the right men in her life. I know what the love of those two lugheads have done for me and that's what I want for my friend. Do you understand that you hold her life, quite literally, in your hands? Are you prepared to take on that responsibility? To be there for her when she says she's fine, when all she really wants is for you to hold her until it's true? Are you ready for the tears that flow for no apparent reason? Are you sure you can handle the glass wall she's put up to keep her heart safe— the one that lets you see her, but not really reach inside? It's made of ice you know, and the only way in is to melt it with love—well, and really hot sex."

Mitch was relieved to hear that small bit of humor finally surface because this was the Kat he knew how to deal with.

"Kat, I have no idea how my friends over there got so damned lucky, but I'm telling you, I've been in a thousand jams with them, and they sure as hell didn't earn it by being angels." He took a deep breath and squeezed her dainty hand, overwhelmed by the love for Rissa he felt coming from her. "I have loved Rissa since the moment she walked into ShadowDance. Her soul calls to mine. Hell, I was a hairsbreadth away from stalking her with all the damned research I did and the hundreds of pictures I sent to Bry while he was in Japan." Mitch sat back a bit and listened, but Kat's lightning-fast wit and intelligence were quiet, she was waiting for him to continue. "How about a bit of quid pro quo? I'll go first, but you have to promise on the souls of those darling babies I see wrestling inside you that you will not tell Rissa about this... promise me?"

"You know I can't promise that. Geez, what if you tell me you are some kind of mass murderer or something? Damn..." Kat's lips lifted on the side assuring him she'd been teasing.

"No, no dice until you promise, and I swear it's nothing immoral or illegal. Deal?" When she finally nodded, he said, "I bought her Granny's house." He heard more than saw her soft gasp. "I overheard her talking to the real estate agent in the diner one day. She didn't see me, but I'm telling you, the sadness in her voice as she made those arrangements nearly broke my heart." He'd released her hand and stood, pacing the room as he continued. "I had always planned to give it to her as a wedding gift. Truth is, the deed is in her name, the only reason she doesn't know is because all the tax statements and insurance bills come to me. I knew she was selling something she loved only because she was so overwhelmed with what had happened, and that's the worst time to make important decisions." He'd stopped and stood, looking at her like a child seeking her approval of his actions, barely breathing waiting for her response.

He didn't have to wait long before she was struggling to her feet with Bryant's help. She rushed to him, burying her face in his chest, wrapping her arms around him as best she could, reaching around her well-rounded middle.

"That is the sweetest thing I've ever heard, and you are so right, she has regretted that decision a thousand times. I know she has, I hear it in the wistful way she speaks about the house, all the little things she could have done with it, ways to enlarge it, decorate it…" When she pulled back, Zach reached for her and enfolded her in his embrace.

"Kitten, don't cry, please. It's not good for you or the babies… or for me." Smiling down at her, he kissed the tip of her nose before moving to a chair and setting her carefully on his lap. "Now, we need to know everything. Time is really of the essence here. Spill it, so we can get you back upstairs to rest a bit before dinner." The twinkle in his eyes promised more than rest, and that was all the prompting she needed.

"Okay, she's at her apartment, sleeping. She just felt so overwhelmed by everything… um… particularly whatever happened this morning. She told me she needed time to think. I was talking to her while she was driving down the mountain, and she'd calmed down some, but she knew the switchbacks were going to be slick, and her car isn't really good enough for her to be driving on slick roads. She wanted to be able to concentrate on her driving, so we hung up. When I tried to get through to her later and it kept going straight to voice mail, I knew she'd forgotten to turn it back on—or at least that's what I hoped, so I called the tavern and asked them to have a look around for her car. They found it and told me there was a single set of footprints going up the back stairs, so they were sure she was up there." When none of the men said anything, she quickly added, "That's it, I swear. I don't know any more than that. I didn't want them to disturb her if she was resting." And then in a voice little more than a whisper, she added, "I know that sometimes sleep is the only escape your mind can have, so it's precious."

Zach scooped her in to his arms and stood, heading out of the room. Glancing at the other men, he said, "That's it, she's resting right now. She's told you what she knows, and I'm worried about her, so I'm taking her upstairs." By the time he'd finished speaking, he was out the door, and they could hear him speaking softly to his wife with words of admiration for her loyalty and smart thinking to have the tavern staff check that Rissa had made it down the mountain safely, and his promises of a world-class foot massage as her reward.

When Mitch looked at his long-time friend and teammate, he smiled at Alex's expression. For years, everyone had worried Alex Lamont seemed to be becoming more remote and emotionally isolated until even his twin had wondered if anything was ever going to melt the ice his heart seemed encased in. So, seeing the love Alex felt for his wife written in every curve and crease of his face was a welcome a sight.

"She's a gift straight from God, you know? I wonder every single day what I've done to deserve her." Alex's words seemed so strange coming from a man who had been as much a machine as soldier for all his time in the

Special Forces. Shaking his head, he seemed to come back to the moment.

"Now, get your asses down the mountain and bring your woman home. We all want her safe, and she won't be as long as she is alone in that damned hole she lives in. We own that building you know... she doesn't know that, and I'd rather she didn't... but we've tried to fix the place up for her, and she just won't hear of it. She insists to the overseer she doesn't pay enough rent to merit any improvements to the place. God has gifted us with a stubborn woman, and it looks like you two aren't going to fare any better." Running a hand through his hair he smiled. "Now give Colt a sitrep and get a move on. Damn, why are you still here? What are you waiting for?"

Chapter 18

THE ROADS LEADING into the small town of Climax, Colorado were getting worse, and the tiny rental car Victoria Paulson had driven from her home in Houston was ill-equipped to handle the treacherously slick, narrow paths that state officials seemed to think qualified as highways. *Good God how do people in this state survive? There must be some special add-on to the local driver's education classes... Yeah, a required workshop called "Crazy Mountain Driving for Dummies"!*

Even though Tori had been born in Colorado, her father had quickly whisked her mother away from her family and moved the three of them every year or so until her mother's family had stopped trying to track them down. She still remembered the words her mother had whispered to her just before she'd succumbed to the cancer that had left her a mere shell of the vibrant woman she'd once been. "Uncle Saul lives in Climax, CO. Don't ever forget that—if you need him, call the Sheriff there. Promise you'll remember... you'll always be safe there." And then she was gone.

Tori had only been fifteen when her mother passed away, and the next three years had been the most tortured of her life. Her father was a mean and sadistic drunk, and he managed to stay drunk most of the time. Tori completed high school a year early despite working two part-time jobs in order to pay the rent on their small apartment and buy food for herself and her father. Donald Paulson rarely worked, and when he did, he simply drank up any money he earned.

A month before Tori's eighteenth birthday, her father had been driving drunk and passed out in the middle of a six-lane highway. Literally in the middle of the highway… without his car. His blood alcohol level had been so high no one knew how he'd been able to drive that far. Why he'd stopped the car and gotten out to walk down the middle of the road was anyone's guess. He'd been hit almost immediately before being run over multiple times. He hadn't even made it to the emergency room.

Tori barely managed to avoid interviews with the investigating officers long enough to delay presenting of any age verification documents to authorities until the day she'd become a legal adult. The investigator who'd been pressing for the information was not happy but had managed to put his anger aside long enough to give her a stern lecture on the importance of furthering her education and helped her connect with enough local resources. She'd always hoped his conscience had been appeased because she knew he felt bad for not pressing the issue sooner.

Shaking her head to bring her focus back to the death trap of a car she was currently trying to ski down a Colorado mountain road, Tori reminded herself all of that was well in the past, and now, she was on her way to Climax to meet with an attorney for her great uncle's estate. She'd been ready to move on when she'd received the letter, and after her phone conversation with the man charged with tracking her down, she was excited to see the ranch she'd inherited from the generous man she'd never met. She pressed a little harder on the gas pedal after glancing at the clock, knowing if she didn't get the keys to the house before the attorney's office closed for the holiday weekend, she'd be stuck looking for accommodations.

As she descended into the small town, she wished she could spend more time looking at the view of the valley that lay before her and less time praying she didn't slide over the edge of the road. She'd never been a huge fan of heights, and this wasn't exactly her idea of a pleasure drive. When she finally found the attorney's office along what appeared to be the town's main street, she parked quickly and made her way to the door only to find the door locked and a small sign wishing her a "Happy Thanksgiving" and saying he'd see her next Wednesday. *What the holy hell? Wednesday? Who the hell takes off a whole week for Thanksgiving?* Determined to find a B & B or small motel, Tori took off walking toward the closest business in town that appeared to be open, the local tavern.

Stunned, Tori sat outside the small bar and grill on a park bench and stared off into the softly fading light. The bartender had been full of information and none of it good. Tori was shocked to discover that while her uncle had owned a fair number of acres, the home she'd planned to live in had burned to the ground several weeks ago. Mr. Full-of-Sunshine Bartender had also told her the only B & B within a hundred miles was back up the same road she'd just descended, and that poor excuse for a highway had just been closed to outside traffic unless you had tire chains due to weather conditions.

When she'd asked about a motel, it had seemed as though everyone in the entire bar had gone completely silent for a few seconds before what must be the entire population of the tiny burg had erupted in riotous laughter.

Tori had no idea what to do. If she tried to sleep in her car, she'd surely freeze to death, and she was so far beyond exhausted, both physically and emotionally, she didn't know if she had the strength to go back inside and ask about any emergency shelters.

Making her way back outside the busy tavern, Tori sat on a snow-covered bench, staring out in to the twilight. She wasn't sure how long she'd been sitting there or how long the tall man, leaning against the post, with his arms crossed over his wide chest, had been watching her with thoughtful eyes shining out from below his Stetson. His shearling jacket suggested he was local and much better prepared for the rapidly falling snow than Tori felt in her thin jacket that had always been plenty for gulf coast winters.

Blinking through her tears, she looked up and felt a jolt of electricity that sent fire racing through her entire body, and she was sure time had stood completely still. For the next few seconds, she didn't even have enough functioning brain cells firing to remember to take a breath. While he wasn't as handsome as some men she'd known, there was something about his presence that rocked her to her core.

"Hello, darlin', what's got you sitting out in the cold, looking like you've lost your best friend?" While she would have been offended if she'd been approached in such a way back in Houston, for some reason, right at this moment in time, it seemed like a perfectly reasonable question. She was so caught up in her racing thoughts, she hadn't even answered, so he spoke to her again. "Darlin', you need to focus here. I'm really starting to worry about you." He'd come closer, knelt in front of her knees and took her bare hands into his gloved ones. When she shuddered at the cold touch, he looked down, and cursing, quickly took off his gloves, and stuffed them in his jacket pockets, and covered her freezing fingers with his warm ones.

Trace couldn't believe the little snow princess he'd found sitting out in front of the tavern wasn't an angel. God, but she was gorgeous—long, flowing, chestnut-colored hair, huge brown eyes, olive complexion, and she smelled like fresh citrus and sage. She'd blinked at him several times when he'd spoken to her but hadn't answered. He was quickly starting to worry her distraction was not just emotional, but that she was starting to succumb to hypothermia as well. Anyone not accustomed to the cold would feel the effects quickly; the wind was whistling through town like an icy knife slicing through the best winter jackets, and the flimsy thing she was wearing was little more than a raincoat.

"Do you need medical help? I can call Doc Woods and have him meet us at his office—" He was cut off by her head shaking back and forth. "You're going to have to do better than that, sweetness. What's your name, honey?"

Her voice was so soft and quivered with the cold so much he barely heard her whispered, "Tori, my name is Tori. I'm sorry, I just got some bad news, and I needed to sit for a minute."

"Well, I think you should be sitting someplace warmer than this." He pulled her to her feet, and she followed his lead as he walked down the wooden sidewalk. *Wow, what kind of town still has wooden sidewalks?* Tori had followed her mind's wandering and hadn't realized they'd entered a warm room that smelled of pot roast and apple pie.

Blinking in surprise when her brain caught up with her nose, she closed her eyes and inhaled deeply, sighing in appreciation. God, she was so hungry. She hadn't wanted to stop along the way to eat after she'd heard all the weather reports predicting near-blizzard conditions in the very place she was headed. When she opened her eyes, the tall stranger was watching her with a small smile playing over his lips, making him look even more appealing.

"Well, welcome back, beautiful, where did you go just then?" While his words sounded almost mocking, his smile reassured her know he was only teasing.

"Oh, I'm so sorry, it's just that is smells so wonderful in here, and I hadn't realized how hungry I was, and it's so nice and warm, and this jacket just doesn't seem to be quite enough for this weather, and I have just about had all... well, I've just kind of had..."

When big tears started trailing down her cherry-red cheeks, Trace was sure his heart had been squeezed from the inside. He stepped forward, wrapped his long arms around her, and pulled her against his chest. He felt her stiffen in his arms before sobs began wracking her small body. Scooping her up in his arms, he headed to the back of the diner. Stella, the older woman who had owned and operated the tiny café for over forty years, hustled ahead and opened the door to her small office.

"I'll get something warm for y'all and be back in a flash. Take care of her, looks like you finally found that angel we all knew Nan would send you." Her words were spoken so quickly, he didn't ever get a chance to respond before she'd hurried away.

Trace sat on the threadbare sofa and rocked the sobbing woman until she finally seemed to have spent all the energy she'd stored in the tight muscles he could feel below his fingertips as he'd rubbed his hand in soothing circles over her back.

Angels weren't supposed to cry their hearts out, and he wondered what on earth her bad news had been, and who the asshat was who'd hurt her. When she'd been sitting in front of the bar, he'd heard bits and pieces of her rambling about a crazy old fart attorney, losing her mama, her long drive, and something about a B & B that he'd found amusing. Tiny Climax had guest cabins for rent during the summer, but since there weren't any ski slopes nearby, there had never been any need of winter accommodations for tourists, so there wasn't a motel anywhere close by.

Once she finally settled down, Trace knew the very moment she realized she was sitting in his lap by the way her entire body seemed to go on high alert.

"It's okay, I just wanted to hold you and get you warmed up." When she started to move away, he tightened his arms around her tiny form. "No, just stay right where you are. You're safe, and I like the feel of you sitting close. You smell wonderful, too, like fresh citrus and sage, light and clean. It's been a long time since a beautiful woman has given me the pleasure of sitting so close. By the way, my name is Trace Bartell, it's nice to meet you, Tori."

Trace had not been completely overwhelmed by a woman since losing his beloved Nan, but this pint-sized sprite called to him in a way that he'd almost forgotten was possible. He was just opening his mouth to speak again when he heard the unmistakable sound of a gunshot followed by screams. He transferred her to the sofa and cradling her small face in both his large hands.

"Stay right here. I'll be back for you. Lock the door behind me and don't open it for anyone but me, do you understand?" He didn't wait for an answer before taking off at a sprint down the hall, following the other diner patrons out the front door.

RISSA STARTLED AWAKE and confused about what had roused her until she heard a footstep in her small kitchen. Jumping from the chair where she'd been sleeping, she crouched behind her tiny sofa and heard a soft curse by a distinctly female voice. Peeking around the edge of the solid piece of furniture she was sure had been in the small apartment since FDR had been President, Rissa was shocked to see an obviously very drunk Rachel Sutton emerge from her kitchen.

"I know you're in here, you ignorant slut, so you might as well come out and let me shoot you now. I'm tired of waiting on those Russian slave dipwads to come cart your interfering ass out of town. Christ, what's a woman gotta do? Those guys could fuck up a wet dream, I tell you. Someone should tie their asses to a St. Andrew's Cross and work 'em over. Oh yeah, baby, now there's a *fine* idea." She cursed again when she bumped into the end table, sending the heavy lamp crashing to the floor. Rissa backed up silently on her hands and knees hoping upon hope the crash had been loud enough downstairs to have been heard over the bar's jukebox.

"Come out, come out wherever you are." Rachel was trying to sing like Glinda the Good Witch beckoning the munchkins out of hiding in *The Wizard of Oz*, and Rissa could only shake her head at the obvious reference to her small stature. Rolling her eyes, she thought it would just about figure that after all she'd been through and survived, she'd be taken out at the hand of a lunatic singing a song summoning short people out into the open.

"Oh, come on, at least I'm just going to shoot you, those other yo-yos are planning to fuck your brains out then sell you to the highest bidder somewhere in the Middle East. Christ, I'm practically doing you a favor." Rachel's speech was slurring worse with each thing she uttered. Rissa felt a razor-sharp edge of fear but found she also wanted to hear more about Rachel's involvement.

Cupping her hands so the sound bounced oddly around the room, Rissa asked quickly. "Why?"

Rachel spun around so quickly, she lost her balance and dropped her gun when she grabbed for a chair to keep from crashing on to the floor. Rissa lunged for the weapon just as Rachel spotted it and fell on top of Rissa, pinning her small frame to the floor. Rissa was grateful for Rachel's drunken state, it meant her coordination was hampered enough Rissa could easily scramble out from under the larger woman. When Rachel grabbed one of Rissa's ankles, startling her, she pulled the trigger of the handgun, and the front window of the apartment shattered. Both women screamed, and Rissa could hear shouting downstairs as well.

"You stupid bitch, look what you've done. Fuck, I only had a few bullets, and you just wasted one of them. Give me that gun, so I can shoot you."

Rissa thought that if she wasn't scared spitless, she might find the other woman's drunken rants amusing. *Seriously? She thinks I'm going to give her the gun, so she can kill me? Just how drunk do you have to be to believe that might become a reality?*

Rissa could hear pounding on the stairs and knew help was close, and it seemed like she was watching the scene before her play out in slow motion. Rachel obviously heard the footsteps on the stairway as well and picked up a small statue from the end table intending to throw it at whoever entered the apartment. In a flash of insight, Rissa knew it was going to look like a weapon in her hand rather than a cheap garage sale statue. Just as the door of the apartment crashed open, Rachel spun bringing the statue up to hurl it at the intruder, and Rissa screamed, *"No!"* trying to stop the deputy who had entered from firing the weapon he already had drawn—but it was too late. Rissa watched in horror as Rachel Sutton sank slowly to the ground, her eyes going wide before she dropped unconscious to the floor.

The officer was followed by about half the population of their small town, but the only people Rissa could focus on were the two men leaning over her protectively. Mitch's voice finally sunk through the haze.

"Put the gun down, Clarissa Jean." When she looked up and blinked, his soft smile told her she was finally safe. Rissa dropped the gun and launched herself in to Mitch Grayson's waiting arms. Bryant pressed his chest against her back, hugging her tightly between them, long moments passing before either man could speak.

Bryant found his voice first, "Rissa, love, my heart stopped dead when we pulled up downstairs and heard a gunshot." He took a couple of steadying breaths before continuing, "I swear you have just taken ten years off my life. I want you to remember this when we get married— my shortened life span is largely due to this moment in time." He knew he was rambling, but he felt her muscles relax, so at least his lame attempts at humor were working to diffuse her tension a little.

"Baby, I swear to God, I'm never letting you out of my sight again." Leaning closer, Mitch whispered, "And I am going to turn your bare ass red hot for leaving the mansion without telling us and getting yourself in this mess…" He hugged her so fiercely, she worried he was going to break her ribs before he finally released her.

Dylan Marshall, the local sheriff, had returned from his honeymoon late last night and had been at the diner when he heard the shot. After helping load Rachel Sutton onto the gurney and into the ambulance, he returned to the small apartment where Rissa's men were keeping her wrapped in her homemade quilts and themselves.

A couple of the bar's patrons had quickly nailed a piece of plywood over the shattered window, but it was still cold enough in the small room to see your breath. Trace Bartell was standing to the side waiting and watching. When he saw Dylan re-enter the apartment, he nodded and left. Dylan had known Trace his entire life and knew his friend had simply stood guard in his stead, never mind the room was filled with various citizens and law-enforcement personnel. Smiling to himself, Dylan thanked God yet again for the guiding hand that had led him and the love of his life back to Climax.

Dylan finally moved to stand in front of Rissa. Looking down at the fragile woman cocooned between Mitch and Bry, he couldn't help but smile. He'd rescued her the last time, but these men would do it better than he'd been able to, and this time she'd make it.

Chapter 19

R ISSA SAT WRAPPED in the quilt Granny had made her as a graduation gift but still shivered so hard, her teeth were chattering. Dylan knelt in front of her, his soft expression made the tears she'd been trying to hold back stream down her cheeks before he spoke a word.

"Well, Clarissa Jean, we find ourselves in familiar, yet new territory." His small smile let her know he was trying to gently tease her and lighten the moment. "Sweetie, we're going to have to get your statement, but I'd like to do that at my office where you'll be more comfortable and much warmer, that sound good?" Even though Rissa knew it wasn't really a question, she appreciated his effort at giving her some control in the situation. His training as a DEA agent would always serve the residents of Climax well.

She nodded, then reached for his arm, her fingers gripping him tightly.

"Dylan… I, well, I just want to say thanks for everything. You have always been so kind and considerate. I'll just change clothes and get my car and meet you down there in a few minutes." When she stood up, the only warning she had that she wasn't going to make it were the black dots that bloomed in her vision just before everything went black.

Mitch saw her weave and watched her knees buckle out from under her. Bryant had managed to get his arms around her and kept her from hitting the floor, his softly muttered "Fuck" echoing Mitch's sentiment. They'd both been so thrown off by her assertion she was driving herself to Dylan's office, they had almost let their woman collapse right between them.

Dylan shook his head, "You two better get your shit together and quick, or you're going to blow this—badly. Christ, how did she come to be back in this cold apartment all alone anyway—no. I don't even want to know. I'm sure you have some lame-assed excuse, and I don't even want to hear it. Now, help your woman get dressed, get some food in her, and get her to my office, ASAP."

Stomping away, Dylan's colorful curses could still be heard as he descended the stairs. Bry looked up at Mitch and smiled, he'd never seen that side of Dylan Marshall before, and it was damned amusing.

Bryant had only known Dylan as a Dom at the ShadowDance Club, but the man who had just stomped out of the room was a tender-hearted softie hiding under a gruff exterior. Something told Bryant, the sheriff would always hold a soft spot in his heart for Rissa.

Looking to his best friend, Bryant smiled and nodded toward the small closet. "Find her something to wear and while I help her get dressed, pack it all, everything. She is not coming back here, it's not safe." Mitch nodded, and they quickly set to work.

TRACE BARTELL KNOCKED on the door to the office at the

back of the small diner. "Tori, open up, it's me, Trace." He heard movement on the other side, but the door didn't open immediately.

"How do I know it's really you? This town is crazy... there's the attorney who takes off a week for Thanksgiving when he knew I was on my way... no place to stay except that piece-of-shit car I rented... gunfire like it's the damned OK Corral or something... Christ, you could be some crazed murderer pretending to be the man I met earlier... Hell, what am I saying, you could still be a crazed murderer... geez, I really need to sleep, and I am fracking starving."

It was all Trace could do to keep from laughing out loud. God she was going to be fun. Suddenly, his life didn't seem nearly as bleak as it had just a couple of hours ago. Really smiling for the first time in years, Trace leaned against the door.

"Well, darlin', how about this—I found you sitting outside the local tavern shivering in the cold because you don't have a coat suited for a Colorado winter, and you had tears freezing on your sweet cheeks because you had no idea where you were going to sleep for the next week. But I can solve all that *and* your hunger problem for you if you'll just open up the door, sweetness."

Trace heard the lock snick, the door slowly opened, and he was struck again by the bolt of fire that shot through him when he reached for her and wrapped his arms gently around her trembling shoulders.

"Ah, my little snow princess, it's okay. Just a little drama in the apartment above the tavern, but I believe both parties will be fine, so let's not let worries about that cloud our thinking right now, hmmm?"

He was slowly walking her back toward the dining

room and settled her in a booth. Sliding in beside her, he kept a hand on her at all times. When the waitress came over, he ordered her a hot tea and the daily special without consulting her. In the back of her mind she thought there was some reason she should protest his presumptuous behavior, but she was so exhausted, she couldn't worry about anything other than being able to feed herself when the food arrived.

"Come here." He gently pulled her against his shoulder. "You have that chalky look that tells me you are just a breath or two from collapse, and I'd like to have you close when that happens." He'd no more than gotten the words out when he saw her eyes roll up, and she looked like a puppet whose strings had been cut.

"Yep, saw that one coming..." He softly laughed as he pulled her up on to his lap and gently laid her cheek against his chest. God, but she felt perfect against him. He was taking her home with him, it was just that simple. It was convincing her he wasn't a mass murderer that might prove to be the challenge. Looking around the small diner, he decided he was fairly sure he could find a character witness or two when the time was right. But for the next few minutes, he just wanted to savor the feel of the soft bundle in his arms.

RISSA FINALLY REALIZED she was moving, and somewhere in the far reaches of the darkness surrounding her was an awareness of a motor and softly playing music. When her stomach growled loudly, she heard soft chuckles.

"I'll call the diner and have them send something to

Dylan's office for her to eat." Mitch sounded amused when he added, "She's going to need her strength to get through all the questions they'll have for her and I don't want to delay getting this done."

"Yes, this will likely take some time." Bryant's voice was quiet but sounded farther away which meant he was driving. "Hell, you know how this goes, they'll ask the same damned questions fifty times to try to pull every detail from her." She could hear the note of sadness in his voice. "Hell, she'll be lucky to get to rest again for hours." Rissa tried to open her eyes, but for the life of her she couldn't seem to pry them open. Giving up, she decided to rest a couple more minutes, surely, that would be all it would take to recharge her.

"Come on, baby, time to rise and shine. We need to get you into Dylan's office, so he and his deputies can ask all their blasted questions. When they're finished, we'll take you back to Bry's condo for the night." Mitch was sure they'd be too spent to make the drive back up the mountain after finishing up with Dylan.

Shaking her shoulder, he put his lips against hers and decided maybe arousal was the way to go. When she moaned against his mouth, he knew he was getting through to her. Pulling back, he spoke against her soft lips, almost losing himself in their silky sweetness. "Come on now, let's get this done. Bry has already called the diner for some soup and sandwiches. Let's get you fed and debriefed, so we can go take a nice long soak in the hot tub, what do you say?"

Rissa slowly opened her eyes and gave him a sultry smile. "Okay, but that's bribery, you know." When he only smiled, she said, "I just didn't want you to think you'd gotten away with it. I don't understand why I'm so tired.

What happened? I feel someone let the air out of me all the sudden."

"Adrenaline crash, baby. I've seen it thousands of times—your body goes into fight-or-flight mode and gets flooded with Mother Nature's own Powerade, and when it subsides, look out floor, here you come!" Chuckling to himself, Mitch remembered all the newbies he'd seen drop like stones just like Rissa had back at her studio. And speaking of that hole in the wall she called an apartment, they just as well tell her now that she'd moved.

"Baby, we've packed you up, you won't be returning to your apartment at least until this is all resolved, it's not safe." He put his hand up when she started to protest. "Think about it, baby… there is only one exit, no security system, you live there alone—because God knows there isn't room in there for another person, let alone two men the size of yours." Grinning ear to ear when she rolled her eyes, he went on. "Oh, baby, do that again later, and I'll paddle your sweet ass, but all things considered, I think I'm going to have to make that one a freebie." He grabbed her and gave her a big hug before setting her back away from him. "Now, let's go inside, I'm freezing my ass off out here. We didn't exactly take time to dress warmly when we finally managed to find out where you'd gone."

Bryant flanked her other side and leaned close to her ear and whispered in a comical imitation of Snidely Whiplash, "We'll be addressing that small issue later also." She couldn't help herself, she laughed out loud at their antics. You had to love a couple of Doms who could make you laugh about being in trouble after a drunken psycho bitch tried to kill you because she was tired of waiting on the Russian mob to snatch you up as a sex slave.

Yes, indeed, that seems to be a pretty accurate synopsis of my current situation.

Chapter 20

MITCH AND BRYANT had been right when they'd warned her the debriefing might be more interrogation than interview. God, how had she forgotten about the hours she'd spent answering questions after Dylan and Mia rescued her? Shaking off her mind's meandering, she refocused on the issue at hand, hearing at least one member of the Russian mob was already in Climax and that he was waiting for back-up was terrifying. Assuming, of course, bat-shit-crazy Rachel Sutton could be believed.

Evidently, she'd had plenty to say on her way in to surgery in addition to her wild raving in Rissa's apartment. Rissa had told them every single word the looney Domme had said while in the small space she'd called home, but honestly, their altercation hadn't lasted all that long. Rissa suddenly wondered about how all this was going to affect poor Doc Woods; sighing to herself, she knew she was going to have to talk to him about what she'd recently learned. She'd been stalling because the whole idea of him being her grandfather kind of freaked her out, and the idea her Granny had never told her the truth in all the years Doc had been visiting as her dear friend really didn't sit all that well with her heart, either.

After what seemed like forever, but in reality, had only been a few hours, Rissa was released and assured there wouldn't be any charges filed against her or the deputy in what had clearly been a self-defense situation. Dylan promised to keep her apprised of Rachel's physical as well as legal situation. He'd also laughingly told her she would have been done much sooner if her friends back at ShadowDance, including his sweet wife would have left him alone long enough to ask his questions without calling and texting him every five minutes checking on her.

"I told them you were doing fine, but I assure you they are going to want to hear that from you, personally, so please call them as soon as you get to Bryant's and let them know I didn't drive bamboo shoots under your fingernails or use the water torture or anything else their overactive imaginations are dreaming up. Damn, but my wife was wired for sound the last time she called. Hell, she was with Jenna who threatened me with the full weight of the Lamont legal team if I didn't let you out of here within an hour," Dylan chuckled as he stood up and helped her to her feet before stepping forward and wrapping his arms around her in a brotherly hug.

"Go on now, get some rest." When she started to pull away, he stopped her with gentle hands at her elbows. "You did great, Rissa, I'm so proud of you. And not just in how you handled things this evening, but in the way you've managed to rebuild your life. I know it hasn't been an easy road." She considered the Sheriff one of her closest friends, and his admiration melted her heart.

Rissa felt tears fill her eyes, his kind words meant more than he could ever know. Her life had taken so many unexpected turns the last few years, she sometimes felt she wasn't driving the train but was just trying to hold on to the runaway engine as it barreled around blind corners and through dark tunnels. Finally finding her voice, she said,

"Thanks, Dylan… that means a lot to me." Grabbing his hands, she added, "I am so glad you and Mia are back together. You deserve every bit of the happiness you've found." She squeezed his hands before turning to Mitch and quickly closed the distance between them. She laid her face against his chest and sighed, "I'm so tired. Can we go now? I'm not sure I'm going to make it much longer."

Mitch quickly tossed Bryant the keys he'd been holding and scooped Rissa up in his arms. "Absolutely, baby. Let's get you out of here and someplace warm and comfortable." As they walked quickly out of the small sheriff's office and settled her in the car, Mitch whispered words of praise against her ear. "Bry and I are so proud of you, baby, you are our little warrior pixie. Hell, you're gonna give Jenna a run for her money at this rate."

TRACE HELD TORI against his side, enjoying the feel of her snuggled up close. He let her rest until their food arrived. "Come on, sweetness, let's get some food in you, then talk about accommodations." He gently shook her awake and made sure she was eating before turning to his own plate. Once she'd known there was a hot meal in front of her, she come fully awake in a heartbeat. Tori made short work of both her meal and two different desserts before finally announcing she was full. *Damn, you have to love a woman who wasn't afraid to eat.* "I'm proud of you for eating so well, sweetheart."

Tori smiled as a pink flush washed over her cheeks. Trace knew his praise had hit the mark, and it didn't appear she was accustomed to being complimented. Now that she'd been fed, her eyelids appeared to be getting heavier by the second.

"Thanks. Mercy, I'm getting really, really sleepy. Did you say something about knowing where I could get some accommodations for a few days? I obviously can't stay in the house on the ranch I inherited, hell, I don't have any idea what I'm going to do about that. Did you know my uncle?"

Trace was uncomfortable with the way the conversation was going, he'd been trying to buy the land she'd just inherited for years. He'd planned to meet the new owner at the attorney's office to make an offer. It wasn't a coincidence he'd been in town today, but the minute he'd laid eyes on Tori, his entire world had shifted. Now, he just wanted to get her inside his home and take care of her, any talk of land and sales could wait forever as far as he was concerned.

"Yes, sweetness, this is a very small community, we know everybody. And just as a fair warning, the way we show people we care about them is to be all up in their business." Laughing, he added, "I'm only partially kidding about that, by the way." He looked at her with a soft expression before continuing, "Now, I want to tell you that I have a very large ranch house with plenty of space for visitors." Holding up his hand when her eyes went wide, he went on.

"There are plenty of people in here who know me, and I'd be happy for you to check with them, they'll tell you I'm not a mass murderer. I'm a local rancher who lost his sweet wife to a drunk driver a couple of years ago. I live alone in the main house, but there are ranch hands living on the property. There is a guest suite that's kept fully stocked and ready for company, and you're welcome to use it for as long as you like." He finally stopped and looked down at his hands, he couldn't believe how nervous he was. *Fuck, I feel like a nerdy teenager asking out the homecoming queen.*

Tori leaned back and watched Trace's expression. Something about him called to her, his lonely spirit seemed to speak directly to her own.

"I have absolutely no idea why I'm agreeing to this— it's crazy on so many different levels, but…" Taking a deep breath and letting it out slowly, she continued, "Okay, I'd very much appreciate having a nice, warm place to sleep." Smiling up at his relieved expression, she asked, "Should I just follow you in my car? It has everything I own in it, and I don't want to leave it unattended."

"Let's go take a look. I'd rather you didn't have to drive on the roads tonight. I doubt you're experienced in mountain driving, and the road conditions are really rough right now. Add the fact it's dark and you have a recipe for disaster. Let's concentrate on getting the things you need most moved into my truck, then I'll have the guys from the local garage come move your car to their secure storage, so your belongings will be safe." He slid out of the booth and helped her to her feet. She swayed once but seemed to recover quickly as he steadied her with his hand on her elbow. "You're dead on your feet, let's get this done."

Trace made short work of moving everything in her small car to his pickup. *Damn, this is everything the poor woman owns in the world? Christ, what kind of life has she led?* As soon as they'd passed the keys to one of the young guys working at the garage down the street, Trace helped Tori into his truck. Reaching over her to secure her seat belt, he spoke softly to her.

"Let's get you home, darlin'."

He didn't even stop to think about the implications of what he'd said. He just brushed a soft kiss over her lips and quickly moved around the truck. When he'd backed out and was heading down the highway, he glanced over to find her looking at him, her eyes wide with wonder. She seemed as stunned by his words as he'd been.

Well good, I'd hate to be the only one here feeling completely blindsided.

Chapter 21

B Y THE TIME Bryant had driven the short distance to his condo, all three of them were laughing about the chorus of their growling stomachs. They vowed to eat a quick snack before hitting the shower, then crashing. When it had become apparent the food they'd had delivered to the Sheriff's office was going to be cold long before they'd be able to get to it, the men had put it out for the staff who had been called into work despite the fact they all had families home for the upcoming holiday. Both men knew Rissa was beyond exhausted, and that her body needed fuel in the worst possible way. While they'd been at the cabin, she'd told them she had to eat small meals regularly, or she tended to "hit the wall" and drop like a stone.

Mitch had been listening attentively as she'd been mentally debating between her need for food and her desire to just drop onto the first cushioned horizontal surface and fall into a dead sleep. He rounded the back of the truck to scoop her up in to his arms the minute she opened the back door of the SUV.

"Come on, baby, we'll get some food in you quickly. Some crackers and peanut butter for you while we're making something more substantial, what do you say? We'll get you some carbs and protein right away, then work from there."

Her sweet smile warmed his heart when she reached up to cup his jaw with her hand. "You are the sweetest man, Mitch Grayson. You take wonderful care of me, even when I don't really deserve it... and I want you to know I really do appreciate everything you do... both of you."

Mitch stopped walking and simply looked down into the pools of grass green that were her eyes and wondered what he'd ever done to deserve her. He'd been a kick-ass soldier and had done things he shuddered to think about her ever finding out, but despite all of that, he held her in his arms and thanked God above for the precious gift that was Rissa. As he started walking again, he barely heard her whispered, "I love you—I love you both so very much..."

Mitch though his heart would burst from the joy. As they crossed the threshold, he looked to Bryant to be sure he'd heard her soft confession, and one look at his expression confirmed he was as overwhelmed as Mitch. Setting her gently on his lap at the kitchen table, he pulled her into his arms and buried his face against her neck, inhaling the sweet smell of her shampoo. When he pulled back, he could see that Bryant had knelt in front of them, and he was the first to speak.

"Clarissa, I want you to know I love you with every beat of my heart. Hearing you love me, too, makes this just about the most humbling moment of my entire life." Bryant smoothed his palm down the side of her face before leaning over and kissing her sweetly on the lips. Standing up and moving into the kitchen, he set about getting snacks in order while Mitch spent a couple of minutes with Rissa.

Mitch turned her face to his and smiled at her indulgently. "Baby, nothing—and I do mean *nothing* in the whole world could make me any happier than knowing you love me. I have been in love with you since the first moment I saw you. It became my life's mission to show you how great the three of us would be together, but now that mission has changed." When her eyes went wide, he smiled and shook his head. "No, it's not what you're thinking. My new mission is to spend each and every day for the rest of my life reminding you why you made the right decision. I want you to be convinced at the end of every day you are the most loved woman you know."

Bryant's and Mitch's words overwhelmed her, filling her heart with an indescribable joy. She'd always dreamed of having the kind of love that could survive the tough times life sent your way. She'd often envied Kat's relationship with Alex and Zach and realizing she was going to have one just as wonderful was almost too much to comprehend.

After her Granny had died, Rissa had gone into an emotional freefall that led to her being alone downtown in Denver late at night two years ago. Rissa had wondered a million times what had possessed her to think visiting the sleazy sex club was a good idea. But the truth was it was just the last in a long series of bad decisions that nearly cost her everything, including her life. If not for a couple of DEA agents willing to chance their careers and checking out a rumor, she'd have been shipped to the Middle East the very next morning, disappearing without a trace.

Mitch continued to hold his sweet love, but his attention was fully on her haunting memories and quiet reflections on all the things that brought her to this point in life. He was pleased beyond belief she was comparing their relationship to that of the Lamonts. Everyone he knew had nothing but admiration for Alex and Zach Lamont, and their love and respect for their dynamo wife was fast becoming a modern-day legend.

He needed to get up and help Bry get food together, so he pulled her in to a rib-crushing hug, just holding her for long moments before finding his voice.

"Baby, you humble me. I'm honored by your love and knowing you compare what Bry and I want with you to the love shared by the Lamonts, knowing you see us in that light makes me prouder than you'll ever know. And I promise you, my love, we'll do everything in our power to live up to your expectations."

THEY ENJOYED EACH other's company during the rest of the evening. Their conversation was laced with lighthearted teasing and lots of laughter. Rissa found herself relaxing and falling even further under their spells, and more than once, she marveled at how easy it was to love them.

Bryant was so humbled by her love that for the first time in a decade, he cared more about his relationship with a woman than he did about being a Dom, and that told him everything he needed to know about the *rightness* of the relationship they were building. Bryant was grateful Mitch had ordered her ring a few months earlier, he'd been so sure of how things would turn out. Smiling to himself, he sometimes envied Mitch Grayson's gifts, and the boyish enthusiasm that survived years of Special Forces missions was something to behold.

The ring was a matching pair of geometric cut diamonds set in interwoven bands of platinum and gold. When they'd shown it to both Jenna and Kat, receiving squeals of delight and bone-crushing hugs, they'd assumed it had passed muster.

They had intended to wait until just the right moment to propose to her—they'd planned on having a romantic candlelit dinner at the cabin—but after their conversation this evening while Rissa was answering a thousand and one questions, they'd decided the sooner they asked her to be their wife, the sooner they could start building the family they all wanted. They were all three only children, so family was particularly significant to them. Mitch and Bryant had always longed for a woman to share, vowing years ago to treat each and every child born to their wife as their own. It would never matter to either of them who the biological father was, they would both be fathers to each child they were blessed with.

Tonight was the night—they would share a shower, then propose, and if everything went as planned, they'd be making sweet love to their fiancée before midnight.

MAKS HAD BEEN in the tavern when the bitch Rachel Sutton had taken it upon herself to forewarn everyone in this godforsaken place of the Russian mob's intent to snatch the redheaded woman named Rissa. He shook his head, wondering how this job could continue to be fucked up beyond anything even vaguely recognizable. He managed to connect with Petrov before his boss was too far out of Denver, and hopefully, his boss would manage to get a flight back out before some half-assed-alert TSA agent recognized him. Maks himself was trying to lie low until the excitement died down; anyone trying to leave Climax with the roads nearly impassible would immediately draw attention to themselves. He had a room at a local rooming house, so he'd just stay in tonight, and hopefully, his nosey landlady wouldn't be notified to watch for men with accents before he could slip out of town early tomorrow morning.

He'd always felt Americans were more lucky than smart, and the residents of this strange town weren't doing anything to change his opinion. If he had anything to say about it, the big bosses would walk away from this one. Hell, from everything he'd seen, the woman didn't remember anything about her time in the cage, and surely if she hadn't regained her memory by now, it was lost to her forever.

The men he worked for were worried she'd blow the whistle and bring down their local contacts. It seems American politicians want to be involved with the dark side, but don't want to be linked to it directly. Sighing to himself, he thought they were the worst hypocrites he'd ever seen; at least in his country, everyone expected the politicians to be dirty.

Walking into the small rooming house, he was glad to see everyone gathered in the back, discussing the events of the day, so he was able to slip up the stairs without anyone noticing. Had he taken a minute to listen, he might have heard his name mentioned.

RISSA COULDN'T REMEMBER a time when she'd enjoyed a dinner as much as she had tonight. It had been exactly what she'd needed. When she leaned back in her chair and crossed her arms over her chest and sighed, Mitch leaned forward, taking her hand in his.

"What are you thinking about, baby?"

Her shy smile warmed his soul. "I was thinking that I have enjoyed this dinner more than any I can remember, and you have both taken what was a horrible day and made the end absolutely perfect." She paused, and he could see she was trying to tamp down the emotion before continuing. "I needed your friendship and love this evening. Don't get me wrong, I love the sex, and I love that you are both Doms... but sometimes... well, there are times when a girl needs her man... or men to be her friends and her lovers. I guess what I should have just said was thank you. My Granny always told me there is very little that can't be fixed with a smile, a hug, and some love. And as usual, she was right." Rissa looked up through thick lashes to gauge their reactions and was relieved to see love reflected in each of their gazes.

Swearing she could bring him to his knees with her sweet words, Bryant had taken her small hand in his and slowly traced small circles in her palm with his thumb while she'd been speaking. He subtly moved his thumb to the sensitive pulse point inside her wrist, so he could note any change in her heart rate before responding.

"Love, you are exactly what we need. Do you have any idea how long Mitch and I have been looking for you?" And there it was, the spike in her heartbeat he'd been hoping for. *Perfect*. It was nice to know she was as affected by them as they were by her. "You have brought hope and light into both of our lives in ways you can't begin to imagine."

Rissa looked up quickly, astonished by what she'd heard. "But I haven't done anything, really."

"Oh but, baby, you have done everything." Smiling at

her confusion, he squeezed her hand and continued, "You have shown us that our perfect woman is brave beyond our wildest expectations. You managed to survive the Russian mob twice and faced a public punishment in a BDSM club without batting an eye. You're smart as a whip—you kept your cool and single-handedly took out a drunken, crazed woman intent on killing you. You're loyal—your friends have been making us crazy trying to get to you to help, and that commitment is a reflection of how you've been there for them, time and time again."

Rissa lowered her eyes, but Mitch wasn't going to let her sell herself short by denying anything he'd said. Taking her chin in his hand, he gently brought her face up until her eyes met his.

"Baby, you have blessed us and everyone who knows you. Don't underestimate yourself. Your sweet Granny was right, you know. Any help you need is right beside you. All you have to do is ask, we'll give you anything you need. You need an evening of fun and friendship? It's yours."

Bryant added, "You need a hug or to be held while you cry tears you can't explain? It's yours. And, love, when you need the strength of your Doms? It's always at your fingertips." Then smiling that devilish grin Rissa was coming to recognize as his *I'm going to distract you* smile, he added, "You need to focus? Well then, pet, your bare ass is ours."

Rissa hadn't even realized she'd been crying until she hiccupped a giggle, and Bryant reached over and wiped the tears from her wet cheeks.

"God, but I love you two something fierce, but right at this moment I need a shower, and then I've got some hugs to collect... well, hugs and more."

Mitch appreciated that Bry had been able to lighten the mood a bit. They quickly cleared their kitchen mess, and he was thrilled with the way Rissa seemed to fit between them. She fell into their well-choreographed work pattern as if she'd been doing it for years. He and Bry spent a lot of time and money fixing up the master bath and bedroom in Bryant's condo, and he was sure Bry was as anxious for Rissa to see it as he was.

Hell, the shower alone was worth the price of admission. The end walls were barely visible for all the natural vegetation growing over them. The long wall opposite the door was one-way glass looking out the back of the condo toward the mountains, and the view was breathtaking. The ceiling of the shower was divided into three sections of rain showerheads, and the lighting could be adjusted from day spectrum to candlelight with the twist of a dial.

There were numerous hidden speakers throughout the condo, including the shower. He and Bry both enjoyed music and understood its power to build or influence a person's mood. They'd made sure they would be able to romance their perfect woman someday. He'd never regretted the time and expense they'd spent on the master suite, and now that they had Rissa, he was thrilled with the things they'd done.

They'd learned a great deal along the way, so when they started updating Rissa's grandmother's house, they'd make fewer mistakes. *Hopefully.* They'd laughed many times at how they'd learned by trial and error—mostly error, very expensive errors.

Walking up the thickly carpeted stairs, Rissa was struck by how richly decorated the condo was for a bachelor pad, it was absolutely stunning in its perfection. "Who did your decorating? It's amazing."

Bryant flashed Rissa a brilliant smile. "Thank you, sweetness, Mitch and I have spent a lot of time trying to get this place ready for you." When he saw her confusion, he added, "We knew our perfect woman was out there, and that it was just a matter of time until we found her, and we were right."

God, if they don't stop saying those sweet things, I'm going to be a puddle on the floor, I swear it. "Well, I think it's perfect. It's just the right combination of masculine and classic good taste. I can hardly wait to see the rest of it."

Mitch couldn't wait for her to see it, and he was sure she was going to be pleasantly surprised to find out that even though from the outside it looked like there were two units in this building, it was in fact all one very large home. The other unit had come up for sale a couple of years earlier, so he'd bought it also. They'd worked to open the two up so from the inside, and anyone would be hard-pressed to find evidence it hadn't been built that way—ah the joys of having an engineer for a best friend.

Of course, a lot of the decorating Rissa was admiring was Catherine Lamont's handiwork. She had taken great pride in helping them *learn* to choose the right linens, furnishings, and *adornments*. He and Bry had nodded in agreement, then promptly looked that one up on their iPhones as soon as she'd moved on in the store. Smiling at the memory, he said, "You know, Catherine Lamont helped guide us, but we've refined our tastes a bit since then, too."

"Oh, no wonder it's so lovely. Catherine is amazing, I just love everything she does. Jenna and Kat are so lucky to have her in their lives." The admiration in her voice was easy to hear, but there was something else lurking there as well. It wasn't envy, but maybe a small measure of loneliness? That gave Mitch an idea, one he planned to discuss with his adopted mama, Catherine about it at his first opportunity. He knew Catherine Lamont would be thrilled to take Rissa under her wing.

As they entered the master suite, he heard Rissa's gasp. "Oh my! This is beyond beautiful." She stood in the center and slowly turned, taking in everything, her eyes wide with appreciation. The natural stone fireplace was the room's focal point, taking up the entire end wall of the room. The oversized bed sat close to a wall of glass, looking out over a view of the mountains that showcased the mountain vista in each season's glory. All you had to do was open your eyes each morning and take it all in. There were three ornate oak dressers along one wall that matched the tables on each side of the bed and the tall posts standing sentry at each corner of a bed so large, its intent to sleep more than two people was crystal clear.

Bryant stood back and watched as Rissa's eyes widened more with each new detail she noted in the room. "Well, love? What do you think? Your silence is making us a bit apprehensive." That wasn't entirely true, her appreciation of their efforts was obvious, but they were anxious to get on with things, so he was hoping to push her a bit.

Stepping forward, Rissa wrapped her arms around his waist and hugged him close before stepping back just enough to look up at him. "It's beyond anything I could ever have imagined. It's just almost too much to take in. I'd be willing to wager the bathroom alone is larger than my entire studio." She smiled so sweetly, he didn't want to spoil the moment by telling her that she had spent her last night in that hell-hole. The thought of her being in that cold, dreary space made him shudder.

Mitch took her hand and pulled her into the bathroom. "Come on, baby, let's get naked and wet."

Chapter 22

R ISSA WAS CONVINCED the shower in the master suite was a gift straight from God. She knew her mouth dropped open when she'd first walked into the bathroom. *Yep, way bigger than my studio.* Her men had assured her it was perfect for them, and she'd relaxed as they'd helped her undress and move into the shower. She decided if it was possible to take up residence in a shower, she wasn't ever leaving this one.

When they'd finally finished washing each other, she'd been so aroused, she could hardly wait to launch herself into their enormous bed, but they'd patted her dry so gently… and so damned slowly, she'd wanted to screech at them to get on with it.

Now that they were finally moving into the bedroom, her arousal was starting to fog her thinking, and her focus was narrowing to a pinpoint where nothing mattered but being fucked. She was so intent on her need, she didn't even notice Bry slip from the room.

Mitch knew Rissa was close enough to the edge he was going to be able to make her come just by kissing her, and he fully intended to keep her so completely distracted and focused on him she wouldn't notice Bry slipping out of the room to retrieve her ring from their office safe. As he'd left, Bry flipped a switch, and the gas fireplace in the bedroom had sprung to life. The ambiance of firelight in the bedroom was nice; it wasn't the candlelight they'd originally envisioned, but this was certainly going to be good enough since neither of them could wait to get their ring on her finger.

Mitch kissed her with an abandon that left Rissa reeling. His mouth slid over hers with such ease, it was as if they had practiced the move a thousand times. He traced the tip of his tongue along the seam of her lips, and when she welcomed him, he stormed in, and she wondered for a few seconds if he was trying to crawl inside and touch her soul. Rissa felt her pussy gush with her juices and the familiar tingling begin deep in her core. When Mitch slipped his hand around her and grabbed her ass, pulling her aching pussy closer to his hot cock, she was lost. The first wave of her orgasm caught her completely off guard with its intensity. Rissa felt like she'd been tossed into a churning sea as wave after wave of pure pleasure moved through her entire body, until finally, just as she could feel herself starting to surface, Mitch slid his fingers through her pussy lips and pressed down directly on her clit and whispered, "Again," in her ear, and her body instantly obeyed. This time she screamed her release, calling out both Mitch and Bryant's names.

Bryant walked back into the room just as Rissa called out his name while in the throes of her pleasure, and it touched his soul that she would call his name even though he hadn't been the one to send her over into orgasm. Coming to lie along her other side, he slid his fingers alongside her beautiful face, whispering sweet words of praise. Once her focus appeared to have returned, Bryant scooped her up, and they moved to the small settee in front of the fire.

Pulling a soft quilted coverlet from the back, they wrapped it around her to ward off the chill before settling her on his lap so she faced Mitch. They each took one of her dainty hands in their own, but it was Bryant who spoke first.

"Rissa, you are the light that fills the darkness of my soul, I promise to make each and every day an adventure if you'll do me the honor of being my wife."

Rissa gasped her surprise but didn't have time to respond before Mitch spoke quietly.

"Baby, you are the answer to a million prayers I've sent out to the Universe—knowing you were out there somewhere and praying we'd find you. Marrying us won't be the easiest thing you've ever done, but we'll be loyal to you forever, and we'll spend our entire lives working together to make sure you know you are loved beyond measure and cherished as the treasure you are. Since I'm older than Bry, you'll be married to me on paper, but we'll both be your husbands in every possible way. We want to build a life and family around you. We'll love any and all children we're blessed with regardless of which of one us is the biological parent. But above all else, it's important you know, *you* will always be the center of our world. We'll be difficult at times, but we'll always love you... we'll be separated by work at times, but we'll always count every second until we're together again... you'll want to strangle us a lot of the time, but we hope you'll remember the depth of our love and respect for you, and that will give you the strength and patience to wait for us to regain our footing." Mitch's gaze hadn't left hers the entire time he'd been speaking, but he finally reached into his lap and lifted a small velvet box and opened it.

Rissa was still trying to process that they were proposing to her. She'd barely had time to take in all of their sweet words when she was suddenly looking at the most amazing ring she had ever seen; she gasped her surprise, then covered her mouth with her left hand.

Mitch pulled on her wrist, saying, "Oh, baby, that hand looks awfully naked, let me hold it for you while your other fiancé decorates it." Bryant took the ring from the box and slid it onto her finger.

Bryant looked up at her, his expression unsure as he asked, "Love? Are you going to make us the happiest men in the world by accepting our proposal?" Then smiling a nervous grin, he added, "You haven't exactly answered the question yet, you know, pet."

Rissa turned on Bryant's lap to wrap her arms around his neck and hugged him so tight, she wondered if he was able to breathe. "Oh God, yes! I love you so much." Then switching her focus to Mitch, she launched herself at him, hugging him with equal fervor.

"I love you more than I ever thought I could love anyone. Marrying you will be the best thing that's ever happened to me. I want you to both know, I'll always love you and only you. I will never stray from our vows. They will be sacred and written deeply in my heart and soul."

Bryant thought his heart would burst at her sweet response, and just for an instant, he stilled, wondering when he had gone from Dom to sap, but he quickly tossed the question aside when he remembered the positive changes he'd seen in Alex Lamont when Katarina has come into his life. Framing her delicate face in his large hands, he looked deeply into the pools of green that were her eyes.

"Love, we want to be married as quickly as possible and as of this moment, no more birth control measures, understand?"

Fat tears ran down Rissa's cheeks, and she just nodded. When he raised his eyebrow at her, she flushed and answered, "Yes, Master, I understand."

Mitch turned her, so he could see her expression. "Baby, you do want to have our children, don't you? You know we won't force you, but it's something we both want very much."

Rissa quickly reached for his hands. "Oh, Mitch I want that with all my heart. These are tears of joy, nothing else." Just as she was about to speak again, Mitch's phone rang, the *Gunsmoke* theme song was a dead giveaway that the Sheriff Dylan Marshall was the caller.

Mitch answered immediately with a brusque, "Talk to me."

MAKS QUICKLY PACKED his bags and loaded them into his car. He'd decided to take a chance on the icy mountain roads, and the hair on the back of his neck had been standing up as he'd made his way up the carpeted stairs. He'd learned years ago to trust his instincts. He'd left more than enough cash on the bed to cover his bill and also a thank-you note for his landlady. There was no reason to give her cause to call the local police and set them on his tail for a couple hundred dollars. She'd been kind to him and let him stay longer than he'd originally requested the room since there were no motels locally. He'd told her his business had been taking longer than expected which had been true enough.

With one last peek out the front window, he noticed a car sitting across the street with men sitting inside. He'd seen it when he'd first arrived back at his room, and now he was grateful he parked his car around the corner and loaded his bags using the back walkway.

The clouds covering the moon and stars made the night inky black, and Maks was thankful for that additional advantage. He quickly made his way down the back stairs as soon as the other guests had settled in for the night and slipped into the backyard, making his way silently to his car.

As he started out of town, he tried to call Petrov, but the phone was answered by another voice. Knowing instantly his boss was in custody, Maks immediately gave his phone a toss out the window. He sure as hell wasn't going to give them a phone number and signal to track. He knew he was on his own until he could get another phone and contact the emergency number he'd been given. The illustrious Senator Ives wasn't going to be pleased, but that was just too fucking bad. The asshat could help Maks or suffer the consequences. They'd only met twice, but the man was little more than a worthless weasel in Maks' view.

Senator Dan Ives was an opportunistic bastard who only cared about himself and money. The man never batted an eye about the source of the money he was *earning* by providing law enforcement and military intelligence to human traffickers. But weasel or not, his contacts would be valuable now.

RISSA COULD FEEL the tension coming off Mitch much like one felt heat coming off a sidewalk in July, but his tone of voice varied little.

"So, you caught one, but the one who was staying at Berta's is in the wind? Well, he can't have gotten far, I assume you aren't giving up? The other one talking yet? Well, keep us posted, please. And, Dylan, thanks for calling. I know you're frustrated, but even the best officers make mistakes. Try to remember we were all rookies once." He gave a small chuckle before hanging up and updating Rissa and Bryant on the situation. After they'd discussed it and they'd each vented their chagrin that Nikolai Petrov was claiming Diplomatic Immunity, the conversation returned to marriage.

Bryant pulled her over, so she was sitting on his lap, Mitch immediately moving to sit close-by, lifting her feet and settling them on his lap. Bryant's hand moved in slow circles over her lower back for several quiet minutes.

"Love, we would like to get married right away, but if you have your heart set on a large wedding... well, then that's what you should have." Sighing softly, his smile was tentative, almost shy. Rissa was surprised to see this side of the ever-confident, in-charge Bryant Davis.

Looking between the two men she loved more than life itself, Rissa chose her words carefully. "I know that it is supposed to be every little girl's dream—the big wedding complete with a dozen attendants, an expensive dress, enough flowers to fill a greenhouse, and a cake sporting multiple levels and a waterfall—but that's never what I envisioned." She took a deep breath. "All I ever wanted was a man who loved me as much as I loved him and wasn't ashamed of being seen with me in public."

Mitch's and Bryant's jaws both dropped. Nothing she could have said would have surprised them more. Could she really be that clueless as to her appeal? Mitch leaned toward her.

"Baby, I want to get a clarification here, because it sounded to me like you don't feel worthy, and I'm really not liking the sound of that so much."

Bryant's low growl was the only outward sign of the deeply seated disapproval she could feel coming off him in waves. Rissa didn't look away from his penetrating gaze.

"It's not that... it's just that all the fluff was never what I wanted. I wanted to love and to be loved. Don't get me wrong, I'm going to have a blast as Jenna's bridesmaid, but I don't want to lose myself in a bunch of wedding planning. I would be much happier with a private ceremony out in a meadow and a barbecue afterward to celebrate with our friends." She had taken both their hands in hers as she continued.

"When my mom left me with Granny... well, it was such a mixed blessing. I missed mom so much, and the feeling of being abandoned was tough. But honestly, it was the best gift she'd ever given me because I had a stable home for the first time in my life."

Bryant squeezed her hand, hoping to banish the melancholy that had dimmed her enthusiasm, he wanted to put the joy back in eyes.

"A meadow, huh? I like that idea very much, pet, but right now, I'm afraid all the meadows have several feet of snow over them, but there's a small clearing at the back of the gardens at The Club that would be perfect. Would you be willing to let Mitch and I plan this for you? Because of work obligations, none of us can get away for a proper honeymoon right now, but we promise to take you anywhere you want to go as soon as we can arrange it."

"That would be perfect. And if it's alright with you, I'd like a chance to talk to Doc and see if he would be willing to give me away." She hadn't resolved all the conflicting emotions she felt regarding the crotchety old doctor, but she knew facing it was the only way she could heal.

Looking between them, she was once again overwhelmed by how blessed she felt, and she made no effort to stem the tears running down her face. "I'm so happy I can't sit still." She wiggled her ass over Bryant's rapidly responding cock before flashing him an innocent smile.

"Love, that sweet smile, heart melting as it is, will not be enough to convince me you aren't fully aware of the effect your wiggling is having on my cock." Bryant looked up at Mitch, and the silent communication that seemed to pass between them made Rissa's breathing hitch.

"That's right, pet, your anticipation level feeds our desire to show you new ways we can command your body. Now, stand, move to the center of the room, spread your feet shoulder width apart and place your hands on the back of your head."

Wow, no gentle buildup, just straight to full-on Dom in a fraction of a second. Rissa slowly moved to the center of the room and got in to position. She could feel her pussy pulsing and knew her juices would be dripping to the floor in a matter of seconds. *Nothing embarrassing about that... right, Clarissa Jean. Now focus and don't mess this up or these two gorgeous men might decide you aren't worth the effort.* Rissa hadn't even seen Mitch move, so his sharp swat to her ass startled her.

"Baby, we will never decide we don't want you. And seeing your pussy weeping for us is a major turn-on, so you just concentrate on *feeling* and less on worrying, or you're going to find yourself over my lap getting another *focus paddling.*" Mitch watched as his words caused Rissa's breathing to hitch, and he knew her pulse rate had sped up by watching the base of her throat. "Now, how soon can you be ready to be married?"

Of all the things Rissa might have guessed he was going to ask, this question wasn't high on the list… especially at this particular moment. *Damn it all to hell, how am I supposed to concentrate when I'm so horny, I can't even think straight?*

"Um… the only people I want to talk to in advance are Kat and Jenna. And… umm… Doc, so… oh geez, this is really not a good time for me to be thinking…" Rissa didn't get to finish because Mitch scooped her up, and she found herself draped over his lap before she'd even had time to blink.

"Spread your legs apart, baby, I'm going to help you with this little concentration problem that's such a distraction." When her legs were far enough apart, she knew Bryant would have a clear view of her exposed pussy from where he was leaning against the fireplace, watching. She gasped at the quick, stinging swats, but by the third stroke she was so close to coming, she was teetering on the edge.

Bryant was watching Rissa and was grateful she couldn't see him grinning like a fool. Mitch was paddling the globes of her ass, and it was quickly turning a nice, warm pink. Bryant could see her juices running out from between the swollen petals of her pussy, and he could hear her soft moans. He nodded to Mitch as he stepped forward, and using his Dom voice, he commanded her orgasm.

"Come for us, love."

Rissa was stunned by the strength of her orgasm. She couldn't believe she'd come from a spanking and Bryant's firm command. Wave after pulsing wave of pleasure washed over her, and when it finally faded, she lay limply over Mitch's lap. As usual, they'd given her pleasure that seemed to rock her entire world with an intensity she'd only read about in books and had never dared dream she'd be lucky enough to experience personally.

Chapter 23

B RYANT PULLED HER to her feet and moved her back to the middle of the room. "All right now, love, back into position with you." When Rissa was back as she had been before, he leaned forward and swiped his tongue over both of her nipples then blew puffs of air over them until they tightened into hard peaks. "Very pretty, pet. I can hardly wait to decorate these beauties. But even more than that, I can't wait to see our child nursing here, knowing you are providing for our child in the way God intended. Getting you pregnant is going to be a priority for us, and just so you know, we plan to be quite focused on *Project Baby*. We've already been reading up."

Rissa had to smile when he grinned at her. He looked so much younger when he smiled, it never ceased to take her breath away.

"Now, about that wedding, my love. How soon because we have all the paperwork done, and we have your dress and shoes." Rissa's head snapped up, and her eyes rounded.

"Really? You have everything already? Wow. You guys are amazing!" She was blown away by everything they'd done for her. She'd been on her own for so long, it was just out of her realm of imagination for anyone to take care of her like this. Her heart swelled with the realization she wasn't going to be responsible for every small detail any longer.

"Well, I can be ready immediately in that case. Well, if you could make sure Kat and Jenna are available to stand up with me, I'll be there with bells on. I'll call Doc tomorrow, as well." She smiled at them both, then closed her eyes and moaned as Bryant dragged his fingers through her soaking pussy lips. "Oh God, that feels so good."

Bryant had already set it up with her friends, but he wasn't telling her that just yet. "All right, but now, about that 'bells on' comment. We also want to collar you, but you need to know that when we do, it'll be at The Club, and you won't be wearing bells—or anything else for that matter. Are you ready to be naked in front of the entire Club, pet?" Bryant pushed his fingers deep as he was talking and felt her pussy walls contract in a rolling pulse at his words.

"I think someone likes that idea, Master Mitch. Hmmmm, seems our fiancée is anxious to be naked and at her Masters' command in front of our friends." He'd kept his voice pitched low and controlled, but he was secretly thrilled with this development. As soon as she was pregnant, they wouldn't share her visually anymore—those physical changes would be for their eyes only—but until then, they planned to enjoy some public playtime. Bryant stepped up in front of Rissa and looked down into her heart-shaped face.

"We're going to love you well, pet, but right now, we're going to fuck you." He picked her up and said, "Wrap your legs around me and slide down on my cock."

As Rissa slid down, sheathing his cock inside her wet heat, she threw her head back, moaning his name, and Bryant was sure he was going to shoot off into her right then. *Christ, man, get a fucking grip. You haven't come that fast since you were a damned teenager.*

Somewhere in the back of Rissa's mind she registered the distinctive click of a lube bottle and felt Mitch's slick fingers sliding into her ass.

"Oh, baby, you are so tight, I'm going to have to get you loosened up before I take you here tonight." When she automatically tightened up, Bryant slapped her ass, and Mitch licked the shell of her ear and said, "Open up, sweetness, I'm going to make this so good for you, you'll be begging us to fuck your sweet rear hole all the time, you wait and see."

Rissa couldn't believe how amazing it felt to be sliding up and down on Bryant's cock while Mitch was stretching her ass. It wasn't long until Bryant moved to the small settee, pulled her flush against his chest, and lounged back, which allowed Rissa's legs to drape off each side.

"Tilt your hips forward, love, present your ass to Master Mitch. When he starts to breech your ass, push out and back against him."

Rissa felt the end of Mitch's cock press against her ass, and she tried to do exactly as Bryant had instructed, but she felt the anxiety starting to build, and when black dots started to appear in her vision and her breathing became short pants, Mitch leaned forward and bit her earlobe.

"Stay with me, baby," Mitch growled. "Remember, you have a safe word if you need it. I'm looking forward to taking you this way. You can do this for me, can't you? Show me how much you trust me."

Rissa managed to get herself pulled together, and in a quick movement that was braver than smart, she pushed back hard against him and felt him slide most of the way inside her. Her ass felt like it had been set on fire, and

Mitch's gasp told her he was as surprised as she was.

"Oh, fuck baby, that felt amazing, but you just earned yourself one hell of a spanking. You could have done a lot of damage to your sweet ass and the tender tissues inside with that little stunt. I'm going to fuck you gently while we make sure you haven't hurt yourself, and then I'm going to take you to the playroom and remind you who's in charge of this body."

Mitch and Bryant monitored her for the first few strokes and when it didn't appear there was any damage to contend with, they set a quick pace, working in tandem to bring Rissa and themselves to a completion that was lightning fast and brutal in its intensity. When they'd all finally settled down, Mitch took her hand, bringing it to his mouth, and brushing his lips over her knuckles.

"Let's go, baby, I want to make sure you never forget we are in charge in the bedroom. Endangering yourself will always be dealt with quickly and severely. Your safety is the only thing that ranks over your happiness, and the sooner you learn this lesson, the happier you'll be… and the easier you'll find sitting down." They led her down the hall to the playroom but stopped outside the door.

Bryant stepped up in front of her, blocking her view as Mitch went inside. Bryant pulled her chin up, so that she met his gaze.

"Love, there are rules you must observe in this room. First, you will not speak unless given express permission to do so or asked a direct question. Second, you will never wear any clothing in this room. Since you are already naked, it isn't an issue, but remember this rule in the future. Third, The Club's safe words are your safe words in this room. And finally, no matter what happens in this room, never, ever doubt we love you and will never do anything to truly harm you physically or emotionally. We'll push your limits and help you explore that bite of pain that morphs into pleasure, but we'll always cherish you and protect you with everything we have." That said, he stepped to the side and ushered her inside.

The playroom they'd built in the condo wasn't as elaborate as the one at the cabin, but it was still filled with equipment Rissa was anxious to try. Some pieces she recognized, others were new to her. Rissa tried to get caught up studying the equipment rather than what they were planning for her.

She had thought it couldn't be all that serious of a punishment since all she'd done was push back because she was anxious to get him inside her ass, but from the array of items he was pulling from the armoire and arranging, she was beginning to get nervous. Mitch finally turned and faced Rissa.

"Come here, baby, I want to get this done. I hate punishing you, but this is really a significant problem because it involves your safety. We've told you every chance we've had, your safety is the one and only thing that trumps your happiness. I think we all agree that's as it should be. Now, I want you to remember this is a punishment, so the goal isn't your pleasure. This is to serve as a reminder of how much we value you and consider your body the most valuable property we own. For that reason, we'll insist you take care of yourself properly."

The entire time he'd been talking, he'd been leading her across the room to a strange-looking hammock device that was standing upright. It had larger holes in the mesh that were obviously meant to line up with her breasts, and it split in two just above her pubic bone. It was obvious to Rissa they had something new in mind for her punishment today.

They began securing her to the odd contraption and Rissa noted there was another piece that would fit against her back, but it was open in some very key areas. Rissa opened her mouth to ask a question, but at Bryant's raised eyebrow, quickly closed it and kept quiet. It quickly became obvious this device was made to be tilted at an endless array of angles, and she was convinced they intended to utilize as many as possible before releasing her.

"Now, pet, you are about to find out why having a Master who is an engineer and another who is an electronics genius is going to make your life very, very interesting." His soft chuckle helped ease some of Rissa's anxiety. "We've noticed you are a very visual person, so we are going to take away your ability to see and anticipate what we're going to do." He spoke in a level voice, but the words alone were enough to kick up Rissa's pulse and respiration even before he wrapped the silk scarf around her eyes and secured it behind her head.

As they hoisted her up, she found herself lost in the sensation of weightlessness. She marveled at the feeling of floating, her weight so evenly distributed, it was like she was on a cloud rather than tethered to some kind of fancy sexual torture device designed by her Masters, just for her. She couldn't help the smile that spread over her lips.

"Well, that's interesting. Would you care to share what that Mona Lisa smile was about, my love?"

"Oh, um, well… I was just thinking about how comfortable this is and how great it is that I have Masters who can design such great sexual torture devices… and just for me, too!" Rissa could sense that they had both frozen in place, and suddenly she was worried she'd overstepped her bounds or worse yet that they really hadn't designed this for her. "Oh damn, I'm sorry... maybe I shouldn't have said all that. Maybe you really didn't make it for me after all..." Suddenly, Rissa was filled with apprehension and feeling a lot less confident.

"Baby, I can hear you, and it was certainly built for you and only you. We were just taken back by your insight and obvious appreciation for what we spent hundreds of hours perfecting." Mitch was smoothing her hair back, his soft touch soothing her insecurities while igniting a fire deep inside that had her juices racing out to coat her pussy.

Geez, Louise, I'll bet they are getting an eyeful.

Mitch chuckled and kissed her forehead. "Yes, the view is awesome, and seeing how wet you are for us is going to make this punishment even more effective."

Rissa felt him fastening something she was fairly certain was a butterfly vibrator over her clit. She was quickly swallowed up in sensation and blinding desire as he slid something inside her vagina, and she felt him secure it so, at least, she wouldn't have to try to hold it in place by herself.

"Now, baby, there is something you need to know about all these wonderful little gadgets we're fitting you with. They are all what I like to call *reactive*. That means they sense when you are just another breath or two from climax, and they adjust accordingly." Mitch smiled when he felt realization move through her. Hell, even with her eyes covered, it was obvious she'd figured out this punishment was going to be about delayed completion rather than pain. She'd be getting a bit of pain, too, because they'd discovered she needed it to ensure her orgasms were everything they could be.

"Now, my pet, it's my turn to add to your introduction to our technological-driven punishment."

Rissa felt him turn her over and raise her in the middle so her ass was high in the air, and when he pulled her legs fully apart, she knew he had a bird's-eye view of her ass. *Oh God, could this be any more embarrassing? Geez, even my OB/GYN doesn't see this much!*

"You know what, love, I don't even need Mitch to tell me you are embarrassed at what I'm seeing. Rest assured, we'll know your body better than anyone, even you, in very short order. And no one, and I want to make sure we are clear on this... *no one* touches you without us being present. Since we know you do your own spa treatments that won't be an issue, but you can be sure, we'll be at each and every appointment you have with physicians for a couple of reasons.

"First, this body belongs to us, so we'll be very interested in your health, and second, it is above all else, our duty and privilege to protect you, and that includes making sure no one ever uses their position of power to take advantage of you. It's important that you understand we'll expect you to be completely honest with us about any upcoming appointments or any incidents where someone has made you feel uncomfortable."

Bryant's voice was almost hypnotizing. She was listening but not really absorbing the information, and somewhere in the back of her mind, she knew she'd likely regret not paying closer attention, but his hands were massaging lube in and around her puckered rear hole, and she was drowning in the sensations bombarding her system.

"Love, you didn't answer my question." Bryant's tone and stinging slap to the fleshy part of her right ass cheek brought her back to the moment.

"Yes, I understand, Sir, but to be honest I'm kind of

drowning in everything right now, so I'm hoping there isn't going to be a quiz later or anything." Rissa was sure she heard Mitch give a snort of laughter before he tried to disguise it with a cough, and it was several seconds before Bryant spoke again, making her suspicious he was trying to not give away his amusement also.

Mitch had known Rissa was struggling to stay focused, but her humorous admission had caught him off guard, and he'd really had to work not to laugh out loud. Hell, the look on Bryant's face alone was worth the price of admission to this play session. Even though they were calling it punishment, it was going to be nothing but pure pleasure for their sweet little sub. Both he and Bryant had always enjoyed the D/s lifestyle, and they would continue to play, but it would always take second place to Rissa's happiness.

They were in total agreement that building a solid relationship, ensuring Rissa never again experienced the loneliness and most recently, the paralyzing fear that had been the hallmarks of her life prior to this moment. Despite what she'd said, she didn't believe it yet, but she would soon; they were here to stay.

Bryant finally brought his amusement under control and spoke evenly to Rissa, "Oh, my love, the rest of your life is going to be the quiz, but rest assured, we'll be happy to remind you each time you forget." As if to emphasize that point he slid a plug deep inside her ass just as he finished speaking.

No sooner had Bryant pushed the plug deep inside her ass, all three devices seemed to come to life inside her. Each one pulsed at different and varying speeds, and within seconds she was panting with shallow breaths, mere seconds away from coming when suddenly everything stopped. *"Argh...* No! Oh God! Please!" Rissa barely recognized her own voice, it was so desperate sounding.

"Baby, remember, no speaking without permission because each time you do, your punishment time will be extended." Mitch couldn't hear a thing from her because her mind was awash with passion, and he wasn't getting anything but complete whitewash from her. He rubbed his hands down the sides of her face, trying to get her to calm down. They'd decided to bring her up and then deny her completion three times before replacing the devices with their own cocks and then giving her the pleasure her body would be clamoring for with a need so intense, she wouldn't feel anything but a pinch of pain that would morph into pleasure before her mind had time to process the feeling once Bryant had breached her tight rear passage.

Rissa gave a quick nod and bit her bottom lip when the butterfly started up first, followed by the vibrator and butt plug. This time it only took a few seconds before they shut off again, and she had to reach deep within herself to remain quiet. She was pleased she'd been able to keep from screaming out in frustration. She concentrated on breathing deeply to focus her mind, not knowing how much longer they'd make her wait was making her crazy.

Mitch watched Rissa struggle to stay calm. Her ability to bring herself back to center was amazing. Mitch knew Bryant was as impatient to sink balls deep in her ass as he was to sink into her hot pussy. With a quick nod, they acknowledged the change in their plans and quickly removed the devices and worked their cocks inside Rissa's heated body.

Without waiting, they set a fast pace that had one of them deep inside her at all times. As Mitch surged in, Bryant withdrew until the head of his cock was the only part of his cock inside her ass, then as Bryant pushed in deep, Mitch pulled back. They continued until they heard the soft moans they had come to recognize as signs Rissa was closing in on her release. Just as she passed the point of no return, Bryant leaned forward and whispered.

"Come for us, love. Share your passion and pleasure with us—let us hear how much you love being fucked by your Masters."

Rissa only heard "Come for us" before she let go and started falling over the edge into a deep pool of pleasure. She heard screams in the distance, and it was several seconds before it registered in her frazzled mind the sounds had come from her. Time lost all meaning, and she had no idea how long she'd been lost in the pleasure, but when she finally come back to herself, they'd removed from their glorious device and placed her on the bed between them. Bryant and Mitch were lying on either side of her, each trying to catch their breath as well.

When Rissa tried to sit up, she felt the bed shift, and Mitch picked her up into his arms as if she didn't weigh anything at all and carried her down the hall to the master suite's large hot tub. As he stepped into the hot water, Bryant started the jets, and the three of them sat for long moments, enjoying the afterglow of the earth-shattering orgasms they'd shared.

Leaning her head back against the edge and letting her eyelids slowly drift closed, Rissa sighed softly.

"No, baby, you can't fall asleep in here... you'll drown." Mitch's words were softened by his smile as he lifted her on to his lap. "God, you are so fucking beautiful, I can barely believe you are going to be our wife."

Bryant moved forward, grasping her feet in his large hands, gently massaged her arches, and she knew then, she was lost. Her Granny had always rubbed her feet to relax her and help her sleep, and as Bryant's hands worked up her calves, then back down to her feet again, she fell fast asleep.

Chapter 24

New Year's Eve

RISSA WOKE UP and realized by the bright sunlight shining into the bedroom, she'd overslept again and for the life of her she couldn't work up the energy to care. She'd always been an early riser, so there was a part of her that thought she should be embarrassed, but a greater part of her was afraid to move. She was fairly certain she knew why she was being flattened by nausea, but she hadn't taken a test yet to confirm her suspicions. It wasn't a secret she'd be able to keep very long from either of her husbands.

God that sounds so amazing... I didn't think I'd ever find a man who would want to marry me, let alone two of the sexiest men who've ever lived!

While she lay back, trying to keep her stomach from rolling completely over, she thought about how beautiful Colt and Jenna's Christmas Eve wedding had been. The entire celebration had been held in the gardens of The Club, and there must have been ten thousand lights that created a winter wonderland unlike anything Rissa had ever seen. She and Jenna had teased Catherine Lamont it was probably visible from the International Space Station, and Hurricane Catherine had promptly pulled out her cell phone and called a senator, who had called NASA and requested they check and take photos. Rissa laughed until she'd cried, and been scolded by the makeup artist when her face had to be "redone" before the photographer arrived.

The wedding had been the social event of the decade in their small community, and no one had been excluded. Trace Bartell had even brought a date, a gorgeous young woman with long chestnut hair. Rissa thought her name was Tori, but she hadn't really gotten a chance to visit with her. Damn, she really needed to be a better neighbor, but she'd been so busy trying not to toss her cookies in front of anyone, she hadn't been going anywhere but work.

Tonight was New Year's Eve, and Rissa had been looking forward to the party being held at The Club. She'd been fretting about what to wear for weeks. She and Mitch had been married in a quiet civil ceremony in town, but the wedding that counted had been the one held earlier in December where she'd been "joined" to both Mitch and Bryant. The dress they'd bought her was the most beautiful thing she'd ever worn, and she'd been touched beyond words that they'd thought of everything down to silk, thigh-high stockings and Jimmy Choos.

Even though they were married, she was looking forward to her Collaring at The Club at the stroke of midnight during the New Year's Eve celebration tonight. Now, all she had to do was get up, get dressed, and find something to eat before she was sick or passed out again. She'd eaten enough soda crackers, she'd wished she'd bought stock in the company because she was sure it had gone up sharply.

Even the checkers at the local grocery were starting to look at her skeptically—yeah, her time for coming clean with Mitch and Bryant was coming up fast… real fast. But she really wanted to get her collar, and she just knew they'd shut down the ceremony if they knew she was pregnant. The Doms at The Club were all super possessive of the changes pregnancy brought about, according to several members she'd talked to.

Oh yeah, her husbands would also have a crap fit if they knew she'd fainted twice in the last couple of days. She was hoping to tell them after the ceremony tonight, and since she hadn't actually taken a test yet, she reasoned she didn't need to say anything just yet.

Okay, it's a lame fucking excuse, but it's all I've got and I'm going with it.

MITCH WAS IN the Crow's Nest as the security command center was affectionately known at the ShadowDance Club, sitting next to Bryant, watching Rissa move around inside her spa, putting the finishing touches on her makeup. There wasn't any reason for her to adjust her clothing because she was naked in preparation for tonight's ceremony.

"You know, she's even more beautiful now that she's carrying our child. Look at the subtle changes that sweet baby is already making in his or her mama. I wonder how long she thinks she can get away with not telling us." Bryant chuckled as he thought about how they'd known for a couple weeks she was pregnant and trying to conceal her nausea from them. They'd let her go as long as they were going to though. They'd heard earlier from Kat that Rissa had asked about fainting and had finally admitted to fainting a couple of times recently.

"She's going to be disappointed when we pull the rug out from under her Collaring ceremony you know. I know I'm going to hate the look on her face, but I'd hate having every man in the room looking at my pregnant wife more. And yeah, I know they won't know, but we'll know, and I just can't deal with that." They were waiting on his relief to show up, then they'd make their way downstairs to the spa to have a little chat with their sweet, but sneaky wife.

Mitch knew the news they'd gotten earlier from Dylan Marshall about the release of both men who had tried to kill Rissa was going to hit her hard, and they wanted to keep that under their hat as long as possible.

"Well, she'll still get her collar but without the public play session we'd planned." They'd already told Alex and Zach about the change in their plans and both men had understood since they'd been in a nearly identical position some months ago.

"Did you find the dress you want her to wear tonight? I don't want her wearing panties, but those big beautiful nipples need to be hidden from view. It's amazing how quickly those changed isn't it? I can't wait to read the rest of the books the Lamonts gave us, and I noticed Kat seemed thrilled to get them out of her husbands' hands." He laughed when he remembered how relieved Katarina Lamont had seemed at the thought of getting rid the books Alex and Zach quoted each time they wanted to restrict her activities.

"Yes, everything is in the closet in her small spa." Mitch was relieved when they were finally making their way down the stairs and moving into the dimly lit corridor leading to Rissa's small spa. As soon as they opened the door, they saw Rissa lying curled up on the massage table, fast asleep, and the sight of her looking so innocent and peaceful stopped them both in their tracks.

"God, she is so fucking beautiful," Mitch's voice was filled with reverence.

Bryant stepped forward and leaned over to brush her hair from her face. "I hope our child has her beautiful hair. It's the color of an autumn sunset, and the curls are the softest things I've ever felt. I love running my hands through the silky length of her locks. I read in one of the books Kat gave us that her hair will grow faster and get really full as her pregnancy progresses." He leaned forward and brushed a soft kiss over her lips. "Wake up, love. That's it, open those gorgeous emerald eyes for us."

Rissa's eyes fluttered open, and she sat up quickly, embarrassed to have been caught napping yet again. Seemed like they were forever walking in just as she closed her eyes. *Oh yeah, Rissa... way to keep a secret.* As she sat up, she felt the familiar rolling of her stomach and took off running to the small staff bathroom in the back.

When she finally felt good enough to stand up at the sink and brush her teeth, she noticed both Mitch and Bryant standing in the small room. Mitch had a damp cloth he used to wipe her face and Bryant had a cup of ice chips. Rissa looked at them and started to cry, big, gulping sobs that racked her already exhausted body.

"I'm sorry, I don't know why I'm crying, but you are both so sweet to bring those to me... I just... well, I'm not used to anyone taking care of me since Granny died."

Mitch thought his heart would break into a million pieces. "Well, baby, I think it's high time you had some TLC then, don't you?" After he'd let her use the cool cloth, he handed her one of the plush robes she used for her clients.

Bryant stepped forward and handed her the cup.

"Here, love, this will help your throat feel better." As she put a few pieces on her on her tongue, they led her to the sofa in the spa's waiting room, and Bryant settled her on his lap. Mitch reached for her feet, pulling them into his lap in what was now a familiar ritual for them. "Now, sweet wife, do you have anything you'd like to tell us?"

Rissa wasn't sure, but she thought she'd seen just a flicker of a grin before it was gone. *Damn and double damn, they know, I just know it… hmmm should I chance it?* She actually considered trying to lie to them, so she could get her collar, but when she looked up at Mitch's raised eyebrow, she knew she was busted.

"Well, I'm guessing you might have figured it out on your own… and I haven't done a test yet, but I think your dream of becoming fathers may become a reality in a few months." There she'd done it. She'd told them, even though she hadn't looked up from her lap, so she wasn't sure how they'd taken the news.

"I wanted to wait until after the ceremony tonight… I've been looking forward to it for so long… and I just thought if I could hold on for a little longer… I know I should have told you, but… well, I didn't think you'd go through with the ceremony… and dang it, I wanted my collar." Big, fat tears rolled down her flushed cheeks, and when she finally looked up, she was relieved to see nothing but love and joy reflected in their expressions.

Mitch cupped the side of her face tenderly and spoke directly to her heart. "Baby, you have just made us the happiest men in the world. We'll be with you every step of the way, and you know you don't have to continue working if it's too much since I'd say it's obvious you aren't feeling that great."

Bryant turned her, so she was facing him and added,

"We are thrilled with your news and can't wait to see the changes our child will bring about in your body, but, love, we are not willing to share the changes we've already noticed with other members of The Club." When she opened her mouth to express her surprise they had already known, Bryant silenced her with a finger over her lush lips.

"Yes, we already knew, love, you cannot keep anything about this body a secret from us for very long." Chuckling, he hugged her tightly to his chest, loving the way she felt in his arms, and when he released her, Mitch had laid the jeweler's case between them. Since Mitch was older, he'd been the one to marry her in the civil ceremony, so it would be Bryant who put her collar on after they made their pledges to her.

Bryant stood up, reached behind the sofa, and brought out the dress they'd bought after they'd figured out she was expecting. Rissa gasped when she saw the beautiful dress Bryant held. Mitch helped her out of the robe, and Bryant said, "Arms up, love, let's see how much better the dress will look once it's on our lovely bride. That's a good girl. Oh, love, you are a vision."

Rissa couldn't believe they'd bought her a dress for tonight's party; it was a stunning shade of emerald green and felt like it was made of the finest silk. It was low cut in the front and showed off her rapidly increasing bust line in the best possible way. It had an empire waistline, so she'd be able to wear it for quite a while, and she was thrilled about that since most of her clothes were already getting tight, and the last time she'd checked she had a whopping one hundred twenty-nine dollars in her checking account, not exactly enough to get the clothes she was going to need.

Maybe she'd be able to hold out until people started having yard sales in a few months. Running her hand over the bump already starting to make itself known, she cringed. *No, probably not.* Well, she could always go to the local thrift store. Granny had taken her there all the time when she was younger. She'd just have to suck it up and go there again even though she had always hated the idea of wearing other people's clothing. Suddenly, she realized they were just standing there watching her as she'd been lost in her own thoughts.

MITCH STOOD BACK and watched the play of emotions move like waves over her expressive face, but the kicker had been listening to everything racing through her mind. Was she serious about buying her maternity clothing at a thrift store because she thought she had to use her own money? He felt like an ass when he realized he and Bryant had been so busy this past month they had failed their lovely wife in a very big way.

"Rissa, look at me, baby." When she slowly brought her gaze to his, Mitch saw a glimpse of the lonely woman he'd first met two years ago. The ghosts in her eyes didn't make themselves known as often lately, and it nearly broke his heart to think their careless oversight had caused them to appear now.

"I think your husbands owe you a huge apology, babe. We haven't made it clear that you no longer support yourself. It is our honor and responsibility to provide you with everything you need, and we'll always make every effort to give you anything you want as well." The wave of affection she felt came off her in a giant wash of emotion. "Baby, we will love taking you shopping for clothing to accommodate your changing body, and we're already working on a baby suite at both the condo and the cabin." His shy smile warmed her heart.

Bryant looked on in disbelief; had she really thought they would make her support herself? He was both amazed and ashamed they had neglected to lay out something they considered a given. Obviously, Rissa wasn't accustomed to being taken care of, but that was about to change in a very big way.

"Love, please tell me you didn't think you had to provide for yourself when you have two husbands who have made quite a lot of money over the years. Husbands who will take great joy in sharing their good fortune with you."

Rissa took a deep breath and looked between the men and couldn't believe how much her life had changed. She'd survived a kidnapping by sex slave traders, not once but twice. She had her own small spa in a Club run by the greatest group of friends she could ever hope for. She had two drop-dead-gorgeous husbands, and now, she had a baby on the way.

Sure, she hated missing the collaring ceremony, but she planned to focus on what she had, not what she didn't have. She smiled brightly at them both.

"I am so blessed, thank you for everything, but most of all, thank you for your strength and love. I am humbled every single day by those gifts, and now, having your child is sweet icing on the cake."

"Loving you is the easiest thing I've ever done, baby." Mitch had also said a multitude of prayers thanking God each and every day for Rissa. "And I can't wait to get you to a doctor because we have about a million questions. We've already made you an appointment with Katarina's OB/GYN in Denver. Hope you don't mind," he chuckled, then added, "Well, we promise to keep our questions to a manageable number, and we'll try to not be as obsessive compulsive as Alex and Zach. I want to you remember, I said try."

Rissa laughed, and in her best Yoda imitation said, "There is no try… only do." She stood and looked at them both for a few long seconds. "I'm so glad you're excited about the baby, and I'm sure I'll be even more excited when I feel a bit better." She sighed and thought about how hungry she was, but she didn't want to risk eating before the party.

"Well, even though we're thrilled you like the dress, it needs a bit of something else, don't you think?" Smiling broadly, Bryant took the black velvet jeweler's case from Mitch and opened it slowly, showing Rissa the diamond-and-sapphire choker inside.

"Rissa, this is the collar that Master Mitch and I designed for you. If you accept this collar, know that you have acknowledged us both publicly and in private as your Masters. This is an outward sign of a soul-deep commitment between the three of us. We pledge our hearts and souls to you. We'll spend the rest of our lives seeing to your safety, happiness, and well-being. It will be our right, responsibility, and pleasure to see, not only your every need, but also those of each child we bring in to our lives. We'll count each moment we spend with you as a blessing. There will never be another, you'll always be able to trust in our faithfulness." Bryant looked to Mitch who smiled at Rissa before pulling her closer to stand before him, holding both of her small hands in his larger ones.

"Rissa, this collar contains gold which is a time-honored symbol of wealth and value, platinum because of its strength, diamonds because they are the traditional symbol of a loving commitment, and sapphires because they are your birthstone and a symbol of royalty. Baby, you will always be the 'Queen of our Hearts.' Once Master Bryant snaps the lock closed, he and I are the only ones who can remove it, and I assure you, those will be rare occasions indeed." As he spoke, Bryant had placed the choker around her neck and was holding the two ends, waiting for her words of commitment before closing the lock. "Master Bryant will close the lock as soon as you have spoken your vows and granted us the honor of your submission."

Rissa was almost too overcome with emotion to speak and had to take several deep breaths before she could respond.

"My body, my life, and my happiness I lay before you. I give you everything that I am... my physical body, my loyalty, and my soul. I'm sure I'll make mistakes, but I ask for your patience and grace as I learn my way." Just then they heard the cheers from The Club's main lounge as the small clock on the wall chimed, signaling a new year had arrived. Bryant snicked the lock closed at that moment, and he and Mitch hugged her between them. The significance of the moment wasn't lost on any of them.

Mitch was the first to speak. "Well, loving wife, sweet sub, and mama to be, let's go downstairs. I believe Alex and Zach have some champagne for us and fruit juice for you and Katarina. They are ready to toast us and offer their congratulations." Moving down the hall, the three of them were immediately surrounded by friends who had become their family in every meaningful way.

Kat and Jenna immediately wrapped Rissa in a bone-crushing hug even as they ogled her collar. For some reason, Rissa's eyes met those of Trace's date, and she was struck by the haunted look in the young woman's expression. Rissa smiled at her, remembering when she was the "new kid" and vowed to reach out to the woman whose shadowed expression reminded her so much of herself not so long ago.

Books by Avery Gale

The ShadowDance Club
Katarina's Return – Book One
Jenna's Submission – Book Two
Rissa's Recovery – Book Three
Trace & Tori – Book Four
Reborn as Bree – Book Five
Red Clouds Dancing – Book Six
Perfect Picture – Book Seven

Club Isola
Capturing Callie – Book One
Healing Holly – Book Two
Claiming Abby – Book Three

Masters of the Prairie Winds Club
Out of the Storm
Saving Grace
Jen's Journey
Bound Treasure
Punishing for Pleasure
Accidental Trifecta
Missionary Position
Another Second Chance
Star-Crossed Miracles
Dusted Star
Lilly's Choice

The Wolf Pack Series
Mated – Book One
Fated Magic – Book Two
Tempted by Darkness – Book Three

The Knights of the Boardroom
Book One
Book Two
Book Three

The Morgan Brothers of Montana
Coral Hearts – Book One
Dancing with Deception – Book Two
Caged Songbird – Book Three
Game On – Book Four
Well Bred – Book Five

Mountain Mastery
Well Written
Savannah's Sentinel
Sheltering Reagan

Enchanted Holidays
The Christmas Painting

I would love to hear from you!

Website:
www.averygale.com

Facebook:
facebook.com/avery.gale.3

Twitter:
@avery_gale